SOFT LIMITS

JODI PAYNE

This is a work of fiction. Names, characters, places, and incidents either are the product of author imagination or are used fictitiously, and any resemblance to actual persons, living or dead, business establishments, events, or locales is entirely coincidental.

SOFT LIMITS: A DEVIATIONS NOVEL

Fans of the iconic Deviations series will fondly recall Bradford as the beloved owner and Master of the elite and exclusively male BDSM club that anchors the series, and also as the wise man who introduced Tobias and Noah.

Dominant Bradford's story is one defined by sudden opportunity, unimaginable heartbreak, and new-found purpose. His calling is to provide a safe and supportive environment for men in the lifestyle. Bringing Dominants and submissives together is his superpower, yet he feels fated to be alone himself.

In this prequel to the series, you'll discover how Bradford is first drawn to Nikki, a beautiful and hungry young man living on the streets, and the unexpected ways Bradford grows and changes while helping Nikki understand a world of strange, new desires.

Deviations readers already know the outcome of Bradford and Nikki's journey together. Soft Limits is a deep-dive into Bradford's story, into what makes the Dom tick, and how he ended up with ownership of the club. It also introduces Nikki, the sub that tests Bradford's patience, steals his heart, and soothes his soul.

To the stunningly loyal, enthusiastic, and supportive fans of the
Deviations Series:

You asked for this book, encouraged me to write it, stuck with me
when I struggled, and waited~forever~so patiently. It's hard to
put into words how grateful I am to you for supporting and
lifting up this series for well over a decade.

This book is definitely yours.

ACKNOWLEDGMENTS

First, I have to acknowledge Chris Owen, who one day, nearly fifteen years ago, posted randomly on her blog: "Anyone want to write a BDSM story with me?" Naturally, this book could not exist without the time, emotion, and energy we put into the series together. Without her blessing, this book could not have happened.

Second, I must thank BA Tortuga and Julia Talbot. As pioneers and leaders in LGBTQ+ publishing, without their forward thinking and willingness to bump up against a resistant romance market back in 2006, a set of M/M BDSM romances like the Deviations Series might never have seen the light of day, let alone print.

And last but definitely not least, I need to thank my beta readers, a trio of great people and hugely supportive fans that read the book while I nervously chewed my fingernails. They gave me their honest thoughts and notes and helped me with important things like continuity, voice and staying true to the series. They assisted with every manner of seemingly tiny details that would matter to the readers that know these books, many of them even better than I do. None of them have chosen to name themselves publicly so I won't here, but they know who they are. Much love and gratitude to you all.

AUTHOR'S PREFACE

Dear Reader,

Hello, and welcome back to the Deviations Series!

Yes, you're in the right place. *Soft Limits* is a prequel. But while one certainly could read it first and not become too terribly "spoiled" for the rest of the series, it's actually intended to be read *last*.

The Deviations series wrapped up with the publication of *Safe Words* in September of 2010, almost ten years ago. I've written *Soft Limits* as an opportunity for fans of the series to revisit some of the supporting characters, to learn more about the history of the club, and to get inside Bradford's head—something that didn't happen in the original series at all.

I quote below a Facebook post I made in July 2018 that says everything I really want to say here. I've copied it word-for-word and typo-for-typo. I wrote this post after a respected colleague called the series "iconic". I was floored, honored, and really proud to have someone say they believed we'd influenced a genre.

I won't call them out, but someone respected and very kind called the Deviations Series "iconic" this morning. I might faint.

The first book in the series was originally published 12 years ago this fall. *Submission* is now available in French (and the rest of the series will follow). The third book was just released in audio last week. People wear pagers and drive PT Cruisers in these books, people! And the only character that has a cell phone is incredibly wealthy. LOL I am continually stunned, appreciative, and gratified by the fact that people still read them, and even more that people still rec them. Wow.

We did a TON of research back then--including interviews with Doms and subs who were in the 24/7 lifestyle. We were given open access to FetLife board discussions. We made visits to BDSM shops and had discussions with their owners. We even had one amazing Mistress who ran her own fetish club put herself essentially on call for when we had questions. People were excited about the books because Romantic BDSM was rare back then. Nobody cared who the pairing was or that the main characters were gay, they cared that their lifestyle was being represented in a positive, affirming light.

We never imagined the books would become what they have. Meeting all those people and writing the series was one of the best things I've ever done. I am so grateful.

The Deviations Series and its characters will always be near and dear to my heart. Writing them deepened my understanding and appreciation for so many aspects of the BDSM lifestyle and the kinky world in general-- sexuality, service, power exchange, care, respect, and the many ways we fall in love—not just once, but over and over, every day.

And as often happens when I write, I learned a great deal about myself as well.

I am excited to put this book out into the world for you to read and enjoy. I hope it prompts you to revisit the series too! And if you're interested in more discussion about the books, its characters, the lifestyle, or just want to meet some fellow fans, come join the Deviations Facebook fan-owned and fan-run group at:

http://bit.ly/TobiasVincentsDeviants.

As always, thank you for reading!

Jodi

SOFT LIMITS

1

The city was lovely in June with the onset of warmer days and summer just starting to take hold. Bradford enjoyed a soft rain shower; it was a welcome respite from the growing heat. A downpour like this one though, was nothing short of a goddamn nuisance.

As he hastily shouldered his way into the local coffee shop to escape the deluge, he found himself longing for the familiar, comfortable, and *dry* confines of his club. With his cozy brownstone right next door, he rarely headed outdoors anymore, except for the occasional stroll to clear his head or take in some fresh air on a nice day.

This was not a nice day, but he'd had an important meeting this morning with his leathersmith that required his presence at the craftsman's workshop, and so he'd been obliged to venture out of his neighborhood. He shook out his umbrella and retreated into the breezeway, taking another moment to remove some of the water from his overcoat as well before pushing his way through the second set of glass doors. He smoothed his hair back with one hand

and sighed as the cooler air of the café and welcoming scent of coffee washed over him.

Ah, yes. Coffee would set him to rights.

There was a decently long line, but Bradford didn't care. He planned to sit in a window seat with the newspaper and slowly sip his coffee, silently cursing Mother Nature as he waited for the weather to pass. Besides, rain or no, he had no intention of rushing home to the club after he'd gone to such lengths to make sure he was covered for an afternoon off. No, he was going to sit right here, read and people-watch, and remind himself that although the nonstop hustle of the city wasn't the reason he'd relocated here many years ago, it was one of the reasons he'd stayed. He really ought to try to get out more.

A couple barreled into the café sans umbrellas. The pair of them looked like drowned rats and were laughing about just that when they took their place in line behind him. Bradford shook his head. He remembered being young and penniless, though not fondly. He much preferred being mature and comfortably situated. It afforded him the opportunity to do exactly as he pleased, which, for an experienced Dominant with particular and often expensive tastes such as himself, was essentially nirvana.

They finally moved a bit, and Bradford took two shuffling steps forward. In front of him was a young man of perhaps twenty, who was tapping a chewed-up pen against a damp newspaper. He leaned around the boy for a better view, curious and assuming it to be a crossword puzzle, but discovered it was in fact the classified ads. He became acutely aware, now that he was in closer proximity, that the young man smelled faintly of vanilla.

Bradford blinked and shifted away slightly, thinking that being close enough to take in a young man's scent and enjoy it was fine in the privacy of his club, but here in a busy café it might make him appear to be a dirty old man.

Never mind that he was one.

"Who's next?" a barista called out and the line moved.

Bradford couldn't seem to refrain from looking the young man over. His army-green jacket was a bit large and hung on narrow shoulders. He wasn't terribly tall and his shoes were worn and soaked through. He had a gray scarf knotted around his neck, water still beading on it in several places.

"Next!" They moved again. Bradford heard the young man sigh and watched him rub each eye in turn with the heel of his hand. Bradford frowned, keenly aware that the city could be rough on young people. It certainly did seem to be rough on this one.

While he was contemplating that, the young man stepped up and ordered.

"Small coffee, black." The boy tapped a granola bar on the counter and dug through numerous pockets but in the end, put the granola bar back.

"Just the coffee?"

"Yeah. Thanks."

"Oh, hey." He leapt into motion, smiling at the barista. "I've got his coffee. A *doppio* for me, please, extra hot. And a turkey club."

The young man looked startled and very confused. "I...uh."

He remained stoically silent until the barista slid their coffees across the counter, followed by the sandwich in a to-go container. He paid, still not answering the young man for the time being, then hustled the boy away from the counter and over to a nearby table. "Sit, boy," he ordered.

The young man glanced up at him sharply with wide

blue eyes. Not just any blue, he noted, but a deep sapphire, and they were moderately terrified. Bradford swallowed hard. "I'm sorry. Please, have a seat."

The young man didn't sit, but after a long moment, Bradford did. He put the sandwich down on the table and slid it over toward his young companion.

"I don't do that," came a quiet reply.

"You don't eat?" Bradford asked casually, pretending not to catch on. The young man was hungry; that much was evident. He was thin and he hadn't yet bolted. "Look, it's yours. Take it to go if you'd prefer to eat alone, or I invite you to sit with me." He set his umbrella on the floor and shimmied out of his wet raincoat, letting it fall off his shoulders and over the back of his chair.

After another moment's hesitation, the young man abruptly sat down and tucked into the sandwich. "You dint haf to," the boy said as he chewed, his mouth overly full. "I ate yesterday."

Well, that explained the sunken cheeks and the narrow shoulders. "Naturally, I didn't have to; it pleased me to do so," Bradford replied a bit defensively and followed that with a sigh. Really, he wasn't fit for conversation outside of the club anymore. "That is to say, I wanted to buy it for you." He watched the young man devour the sandwich, pieces of bacon and lettuce sticking out of the corners of the boy's mouth. He rolled his eyes at himself and touched the edge of the young man's newspaper with one finger, sliding it closer to look it over as he sipped his *doppio* slowly. "Delivery boy, third-shift stocker, parking lot attendant, hm..." Bradford glanced up at the boy. "What's your name?"

"Nikki," the young man answered, chewing still.

"Nikki. I see." He shifted in his seat. "Do you have a last name, Nikki?"

Nikki shook his head. Whether that meant "no" or "none of your business" was difficult to tell, but he assumed the latter and didn't press the issue. After all, he could count on fewer than the fingers of one hand the number of people who knew his own last name.

"Well, *Nikki*." He drew out the name, trying it out on his tongue. "Been in town long?" It was obvious the boy had not, and as Bradford expected, he got another shake of the head.

"I see." He leaned forward, closer to Nikki, who eyed him warily but didn't appear to have any intention of putting down his half-eaten sandwich. "Boys without last names have a very hard time getting work in this town." Nikki searched his eyes for a moment and sighed, his shoulders slumping. "However," Bradford said grandly, much too grandly for a small local café, "I have need of a dishwasher, and perhaps some other errand-type work, if you are interested."

The offer hung in the air between them, and he couldn't be sure which of them was more startled by it: Nikki, who stared at him frozen in midchew, or himself. He most certainly did not need another dishwasher. Where the hell had that come from? Damn those blue eyes. And that soft voice. And smooth skin.

"Christ." Bradford swore under his breath, hiding his consternation behind another sip of strong coffee. *You're too old for such lechery*.

Nikki shrugged, finally. "Yeah? Okay. Thanks."

And just like that, Bradford had himself a brand-new dishwasher.

Huzzah.

2

Despite the rather dubious rationale surrounding the boy's hiring, Nikki turned out to be a very reliable employee. He showed up on time, worked as much overtime as needed without complaint, and in the month that he'd been staffed in the club's kitchens, he hadn't missed a single day.

For his part, Bradford hadn't seen so much of the inside of his kitchens since he'd taken over management of the club years ago. Something brought him in nearly every day now. At first it was under the pretense of checking in on Nikki, getting a report from the head chef, or some such business-related excuse. When that became too obviously unnecessary, he would find other reasons to stop in.

"Can I help you, sir?" Chef asked as he came through the door from the main dining room.

"The boy still seems to be working out, hm?"

Chef looked up from his paperwork to glance in Nikki's direction. "Reliable, minds his own business, follows directions, quite capable."

Bradford nodded.

"Did you have a concern, sir?"

"No, I just...he is of particular interest to me, if you must know, Reggie." Bradford set a tray and a glass of water down on the worktable. "These were left in my office."

"Master Bradford, I am positive one of your house boys can handle such mundane errands for you," Chef teased. "It's their pleasure to serve, after all."

Bradford raised an eyebrow. Reggie had been with the club for a long time and ran a tight ship. He shouldn't have been surprised that the man was suspicious. "Watch yourself, boy, or I'll have to take a spatula to your ass again." That had been a most creative evening.

Chef cleared his throat and was suddenly very interested in a certain form on his desk. "Yes, sir. Thank you, sir."

Apparently, the staff was observant. That wouldn't do; it didn't reflect well upon him at all. So, one afternoon, after teasing a house boy into telling him what time Nikki usually took his break—and then rewarding the boy with a spanking—he decided to have a smoke behind the club. He didn't smoke often; it was an affectation mostly, but he enjoyed it when he chose to indulge. He took a long drag as Nikki slipped out the back door, trying to look nonchalant. He would have failed with literally anyone else in the club except for Nikki himself, as he had no need to smoke outside with the dumpsters.

"Hey." Nikki greeted Bradford with a smile and opened up a bottle of Coke.

"Oh, hey there." Bradford tried to sound casual but remained inwardly appalled at himself. He was *the* Master of this gentleman's club after all—he had final say on everything that had to do with anything and anyone, and yet here he was, making up excuses and stalking this young man like a starry-eyed teenaged girl. "On break?"

"Yeah." Nikki took a swig. "Hot in there today."

It's rather warm out here, too. Bradford took another drag. This felt like role play. It felt like a scene he'd taken pains to set up. A powerful and handsome gentleman (if he did say so himself) and a pretty little twink meet "accidentally" in an alley. Only this was actually happening, and he was certainly *not* in control.

Not at all.

It would be humiliating should any of his contemporaries find out.

"How is everything going for you?" There. That was a reasonable question for an employer to be asking. "Settled in?"

"Yeah."

It didn't appear that Nikki was one for many words. That was just as well—he didn't need to hear the boy speak; he just liked to look. He let his eyes shamelessly peruse Nikki's body. Nikki was shorter, and although those shoulders were still narrow, the boy didn't look as bony as when he'd first picked the young man up.

Hired. Not picked up. *Hired.*

Semantics.

Nikki was petite in stature, had a boyish face, and those sapphire eyes shone so brightly from under unkempt, dishwater-blond bangs that they truthfully took his breath away, and made...other things stir. Pretty to look at. Decidedly of legal age, thank God, but was the boy too immature for...? Well.

"Where do you go when you leave here in the evenings?" he asked, making small talk as he tossed his cigarette on the ground and stomped it out. He envisioned Nikki living in an apartment with several other young roommates, maybe artists or college students, next to, perhaps, a local bar where Nikki would pair up with—who? Girls? Boys? He honestly couldn't be sure. "Where do you live, Nikki?"

Nikki looked up and met his eyes again. "Here and there."

"Oh?" Hm. Curious.

"Yeah."

"Such as?"

"Well, like here." Nikki gestured to a corner of the back stoop. "Or over there." The boy pointed to a flat slab of concrete next to the line of dumpsters that served the club. It was covered by a wide awning. "If it's raining."

He laughed lightly. Surely the boy was putting him on? But Nikki watched him, the boy's face still as stone.

"You...out here?" he stammered.

Nikki nodded. "I can move on if you want; there's a bench out by the subway station that no one usually claims. It's nice and dark there too, so the cops let me be."

The boy was...homeless?

Homeless.

He stared at Nikki, seeing the boy entirely differently than he had just moments before. He hadn't even considered the idea that Nikki didn't have a place to stay, a roof over his head, or a bed to sleep in. "I pay you, don't I?"

Nikki snorted, and the boy's reply was the most he'd said to Bradford at one time since the day they'd met. "Yeah, but...you're joking, right? Wait. You're serious? I mean...do you have any idea what rent costs in this city? I can't afford—"

"But surely you could find—"

"Roommates?"

"Well, yes. As a start."

Nikki leaned toward him. "Boys without last names have a very hard time finding housing in this town." The boy kept his voice low as he used Bradford's words against him, and with that, Bradford's world tilted heavily on its axis, so sharply he knew it would never—shouldn't ever—go back.

The boy's words stung him worse than any flogger could. In one breath Nikki had taken him down several notches, as expertly as a Dom might upbraid a presumptuous sub.

He opened his mouth to reply but found he was unable to shape what he was feeling or thinking into anything coherent. After a long, awkward moment, all he could manage to say was, "I'm terribly sorry."

Nikki tossed that head of unruly blond hair. "Right. I'll come by next week to pick up my pay." The boy got up, putting the cap on the bottle of Coke.

"No. *Wait.*" He barked the order loud enough that Nikki froze in place. "No, Nikki. I'm *not* firing you. On the contrary," he told the boy, speaking slowly, "you must have a raise." He turned and headed into the club through the back door, brushing past Nikki, entirely too humiliated to look at the boy any longer. "*And* it appears that we are in need of staff housing. *And* I really have to reevaluate how I hire people. *And...Jesus Christ!*"

When had he turned into such an arrogant, privileged, insensitive asshole? How had he allowed himself to become so out of touch? He knew better. He absolutely did. He was raised better for one thing, having had no privilege at all as a young man, and there was no denying that his mentor, Harrison, had taught him better by example.

He left Nikki standing and staring at him from the back doorway as he made his way through the kitchen and into the club via the dining room door. He would look into his payroll practices immediately.

"What the *hell* is wrong with me?"

Everyone in the kitchen was watching him as he left the room, he knew, and hearing everything he'd just said.

It was just as well, really.

3

As the door to the dining room swung closed behind Bradford, all eyes slowly turned on Nikki.

Nikki casually took the cap off his Coke and took a big swig, then had a long look around the room. No one was moving. No one said a word. They just stared at him, frozen in their tracks.

"What?" he asked, finally.

The sound of his question seemed to wake them, and he found himself suddenly surrounded by the kitchen staff, who started firing off questions.

"What happened?"

"I don't know."

"What did you say to him?"

Nikki shrugged. "I just told him I'd been...I mean, that I couldn't afford rent."

"Is he taking you on?"

"Is he, what?" Wasn't he already on? "I mean he offered me a raise."

"He was talking to himself. Did you hear that?"

"Hey! Hey." Chef's voice boomed over their heads. "All of

you. Back to work, we have dinner to prep. *Now.* Everyone. Go on."

The staff scattered with mutters of "Yes, Chef," and "Sorry, Chef," until Chef was able to approach him.

"Sorry about that."

"No problem." Well, he said "No problem," but he was actually thinking, *What the fuck was that?*

"It's not often we see the boss all worked up, is all. I've been here a long, long time, and I don't recall him ever looking like that. I've never even seen him lose his composure in front of the staff. That was quite a thing."

Nikki shrugged. "I guess?"

Chef found him a stool and told him to stay put. That was fine, he was still trying to get his head around what just happened. He was totally confused, and he was still pretty sure he was getting fired. It had been a sweet gig while it lasted. He couldn't remember the last time he was able to keep a job for a whole month.

"Are you okay?"

"Huh?" Nikki blinked at the kid who'd stepped in front of him. "Yeah. Sure." He knew this kid. He'd seen him around. What was his name? "It's Brian, right?"

"Yep," Brian replied cheerfully. "Master Bradford says I should take you home."

"...home?" Hadn't they just had this discussion?

"To his brownstone. Next door. He says to help you get comfortable, and he'll be along in a couple of hours."

Nikki frowned. "I don't think I—"

Brian nodded. "He said you would be reluctant but that I should tell you that it's not a contract; it's just a place for you to stay tonight. You'll have your own room."

"Okay, you two. We have work to do in here. Brian, can you finish your conversation with Nikki elsewhere, please?"

"Oh. Of course, sir. Sorry, sir." Brian took Nikki by the hand and led him out of the kitchen and into the large main dining room, which was being set for guests with dinner reservations.

"My own room?" It was really hard to tell if this was shady or sincere. Bradford hadn't given him shady vibes yet, though. "I don't understand."

"You'll see. I know which room, I'll show you." Brian started walking, leaving him little choice but to follow.

"Brian, have you ever seen Bradford like that?"

"Oh." Brian shook his head as they walked. "I didn't see what happened in the kitchen—I was waiting for him in his office. But when he got there, he was talking to himself and he seemed very agitated. I've only seen Sir that way once before, and it was in private."

Okay, wait. So, he'd upset the boss, and instead of getting fired, it looked like he was getting a raise and a bed to sleep in for his troubles.

That was a new one.

He followed Brian to the far side of the dining room and down a long, bare hallway that ended at an ornately carved mahogany door. Brian produced a key and put it in the lock, punched some numbers into an alarm pad, and the heavy door swung open easily.

"Come on." Brian led the way along a much fancier hall with artwork on the walls, up a wide staircase and around the heavy banister. The upstairs landing led to another, wider hallway. "This is it. Master Bradford's suite is the big mahogany door over there."

"Why do you call him Master?"

Brian looked at him like he had three heads, and blinked. "Because he told me to. It's what everybody calls him."

Everybody? He raised an eyebrow as Brian opened the door and led him into a bedroom.

The room was huge and had an enormous four-poster bed in the center. At one end of the room was a large dresser with a green marble top, and there was a tall window at the other end, framed with heavy molding and dark curtains.

"Your bathroom is in here," Brian said, stepping through the door and turning on the light.

He had his own bathroom?

"This chest over here has more blankets and pillows and things if you need them. I think Will is on tonight, so if you need anything you can ring him. The button is there by the door."

"Ring...?"

"Sure. Will is on call for Master Bradford. He'll be hanging out in the kitchen most of the night. In the wee hours, he'll be in the staff bedroom, probably watching movies."

"Bradford has overnight help?"

"Of course. To see to his needs in the middle of the night, wake him in case of club emergencies, bring his coffee and breakfast in the morning. Will has two nights a week, Juno has two, and Cade, Jamison, and I each have one."

"You, too?"

"Sure. I'm on Wednesdays."

Nikki shook his head. Bradford must be loaded if he could afford someone just to be awake all night in case he needed anything while he was sleeping.

"I think that's it. I'm to see to your needs until Will arrives. Are you hungry?"

"No." Nikki shook his head. He didn't have *needs* for Brian to see to. All of this was just weird.

"Can I start a shower for you? I can bring you some tea for when you get out."

"No, Brian, I can do it myself."

"Let me find you a robe."

"No!" he shouted. "No. Thank you. I don't need your help." He really hadn't meant to yell, but this was all so strange, and he was out of patience.

"Oh." Brian suddenly looked a lot smaller than he had a moment ago, and his eyes locked studiously on the floor. "I'm so sorry. I'll just be outside, then. If you need me you can ring the bell. I'm very sorry." He backed out of the room and closed the door behind him, never raising his eyes above Nikki's knees.

He blinked at the door and sighed. Well, that wasn't good. He'd have to apologize to Brian later. But for right now, the door was closed, and Nikki was pretty set on it staying that way. He found the robe on his own, and a bath towel, then stripped and left his clothing on the bed before climbing into the enormous shower.

4

That night, after tripping over himself in a very un-Dom-like manner with another apology, Bradford insisted that Nikki keep the spare guest room in his brownstone indefinitely. The conversation had evidently been far more awkward for Bradford than for Nikki, who, after Bradford's embarrassingly long-winded and heartfelt confession of his lack of empathetic perspective, very simply accepted his apology and thanked him for the place to stay.

Two weeks later, the boy was indeed still in residence, although Bradford had started the ball rolling on the purchase of a small brownstone a few blocks away, which he intended to convert into housing for staff. Nikki had been an ideal houseguest thus far: he proved to be trustworthy, was out of the house working a great deal, and mostly kept to himself in his room when at home, staying out of Bradford's way as much as possible.

Bradford was rather disappointed by that; he would have been perfectly content to trip over the young man once in a while.

He would have been even happier to have the boy

kneeling nearby, but even this many weeks into his employment, Nikki was either oblivious as to what went on outside of the kitchen or had absolutely no interest. As far as he knew, the boy hadn't asked a single question, expressed any curiosity, or given anyone in leather a second look.

It was maddening.

But Bradford had been known to meddle, especially where it suited his interests, and so one afternoon he sent for Nikki. He perched, leaning on the corner of his desk, arms crossed, looking as casual as he could muster, and waited.

And waited...

He glanced at his watch.

Any sub in the club, when summoned by Bradford himself, would have dropped everything instantly and appeared in Bradford's doorway, eyes down and back straight, in moments. Bradford was about to reach for the house phone when there was a knock at the door.

"Come," Bradford called, trying to find the casual stance he'd been working on earlier.

Brian, one of Bradford's favorite young submissives, appeared in the doorway. Alone. The boy sank to his knees right there, eyes on the floor. "I..." Brian cleared his throat, voice shaky and thin as words began to spill out of him. "He wouldn't come with me, sir. I tried to tell him you meant for him to come right now, but he insisted that his break wasn't for another fifteen minutes and he asked me to tell you... he...he wanted me to tell you he'd be here soon, sir. He said you'd understand, and I tried to explain but he...I'm sorry, sir. I'm sorry."

Bradford stared at the boy, momentarily at a loss for words in the face of poor Brian's distraught ramblings. After a breath or two he recovered, blinking away his dismay at having been put off. Nikki was not a sub, he reminded himself, and the boy was likely following the rules that Chef set for the civilians on the kitchen staff. He would simply have to wait for Nikki's break.

This time.

If all went to plan, next time the blue-eyed boy would come running.

For the moment, however, there remained a sub in distress in his doorway. "Brian." He spoke the boy's name smoothly. He regretted having to dole out punishment when the situation appeared to be beyond Brian's control, but the boy expected it, and Brian's current emotional state demanded it. "That is one stroke, as punishment for not bringing Nikki to me."

"Yes, sir. Thank you, sir." Brian's disappointment was clear in his tone, as was his acceptance.

"And a barehanded spanking at the end of your shift for doing your best to please me." Bradford allowed himself a slight grin. That should take the mental sting out of the punishment and put it somewhere Brian would enjoy much more.

"Oh! Yes, sir! Thank you, sir!" All was apparently right in Brian's world once more. "Shall I present for punishment now, sir?"

"No, no." Bradford waved his hand broadly as he headed back around his desk to sit. "Come see me after your shift."

"I will, sir. Thank you, sir!" Brian jumped up and started to go but froze suddenly. "Oh..."

Bradford was so amused by the pup that he let the transgression go without comment. "You are dismissed."

"Thank you, sir!" Brian scurried away, closing the door behind him.

Nikki kept his word and presented himself in Bradford's office on his break. He knocked briefly and opened the door.

"It's customary to wait to be invited in," Bradford told the boy evenly, not looking up from his paperwork.

"Oh. Right, sorry." Nikki came in anyway, closing the door behind him. "You wanted to see me?"

"I did. In the future, if I ask to see you, you should consider yourself excused from whatever you are doing and come right away. Chef will understand." Bradford glanced up from his papers and looked Nikki in the eyes. "Clear?"

God, the blue.

"Yes. Sorry. Okay."

"Have a seat." It was thrilling to have had an excuse to top Nikki just then, even to that small extent, and he felt goose bumps rise on his skin. He stood, intending to resume his casual position on the front of his desk for the rest of their talk.

"Yes, sir."

The boy's reply, however, went straight to Bradford's cock and he sat abruptly, thinking it better that he remain ensconced behind his desk for the moment. He reached for the bottle of water sitting on a ceramic coaster on his desk and took a long sip before relaxing back in his chair. He'd have to do casual indifference from here.

"You have been an excellent employee, Nikki," Bradford began, finally regaining control over himself.

"Thanks, Bradford."

Bradford's lips twitched at the boy's use of his name. "Yes. Well. You're welcome." He shifted in his seat. "I'd like to try to offer someone else a leg up soon, so I think this is an appropriate time for a promotion."

"A promotion?"

"Yes. I have an opening on my house staff, I was thinking

perhaps you might be interested." He actually did have an opening this time; Timothy was being moved into the dining room. That Timothy's well-deserved promotion came about at this moment because Bradford needed an opening for Nikki on his house staff was utterly beside the point.

"The staff. Which means...?"

"Oh, you'd be cleaning and restocking the second- and third-floor rooms, running errands, keeping the main floor presentable. Assisting our members as needed. At any given time, there are at least two boys on shift, three shifts in a day. Shifts are typically chosen by seniority, so I'm not sure which one you'd be on just yet, but—"

"It is much cooler out here than in the kitchen," Nikki observed, interrupting.

He raised an eyebrow. "It's a small raise as well."

Nikki nodded. "I could maybe meet a few more people."

"Naturally. You'd meet the rest of the house staff, the waitstaff, my bartenders, and you'd potentially have the opportunity to get to know some of the members, depending on what shift you work. Also, house staff have a uniform."

He carelessly neglected to mention that the uniform was little more than a custom-fitted leather harness.

Oops.

"Well, okay. It sounds pretty good. Thank you."

He allowed himself a subtle smile. *So far, so good.* "You're welcome." He was finally able to move out from behind his desk, and he stepped around it. "There is some training involved. Have you met Levi?"

"Not yet."

"Oh, you're in for a treat. He's a..." He stopped himself by pursing his lips together. "He's very good at what he does."

Perhaps better not to scare the boy off. The uniform might be enough without more information on Levi—his handsome, talented, and submissive daytime manager.

"Okay, great."

"Wonderful. Welcome to the front of the house. I'm very proud of you." He offered his hand and Nikki shook it politely. "We'll get you set up with Levi soon."

"Sounds good." Nikki stood up, apparently understanding that the meeting was over. "Later." He headed for the door.

"Have a nice afternoon," he replied, and Nikki closed the door behind him with a quiet click. God, how he wanted to get under that boy's skin. Nikki made his spine itch impatiently and his fingers long for a paddle.

Patience, old boy, he thought. *Patience.*

If he handled this right, it would be a beautiful thing.

5

The next afternoon, Bradford arranged for Nikki to be fitted for his uniform. His contracted artisans—be they leathersmiths like Liam, tailors, or even carpenters—typically chose one of the playrooms on the second floor to work. They had privacy and plenty of room to move around. But today, at his request, Nikki was being fitted in his office. This particular fitting needed to be carefully managed, and he didn't think that beginning the boy's journey in a room full of whips and chains would quite set the tone he was looking for. He wanted to do this where Nikki would feel comfortable. He needed the boy to be open. Receptive.

Nikki was relaxed. He submitted to the measurements easily enough, then took a seat while Liam hurried out to his van. Bradford sat quietly behind his desk, pretending to look over a couple of budget reports, waiting for the craftsman's return. It seemed wiser not to warn the boy what Liam would be returning with. It was on occasion better to beg forgiveness than to ask permission, or so it was said, and though it pained him, for the moment he did still require Nikki's permission.

Liam returned with a contraption made of studded leather hanging over his shoulder and some extra leather straps and buckles in one hand. Brian held the door open for him and followed him inside, a small toolbox in one hand.

"Ah, Liam. Let Brian know if he can assist." Bradford suggested.

Brian grinned. "Thank you, sir."

Nikki looked Liam over with a doubtful expression. "What are those?"

"Stand up, please," Liam replied cheerfully. Nikki stood and made his way over. "You'll want to take your shirt off."

"My shirt...?" Nikki's fingers went to the collar of his T-shirt, but he didn't pull it off.

Bradford looked up from the file he wasn't reading. "You have to be bare-chested to be fitted."

That doubtful look seemed to settle into Nikki's entire body, but he tugged off his shirt and tossed it onto a chair uncertainly. "Okay."

Oh, so much better than okay. The boy's skin was like cream, smooth and flawless, and eating regularly had definitely been good for his physique. The leather bulldog harness Liam picked up was black and white: black leather straps with bright white edging, stainless-steel hardware and details, and a D-ring over the sternum. Nikki's eyes looked from the harness to Bradford and back again.

"What is *that*?"

Bradford allowed himself a slow grin, amazed that the boy had actually been oblivious.

Oh, what fun.

"That is your uniform, the chest piece at least. Brian has a selection of shorts for you; it doesn't matter to me which you choose."

"I'm not wearing *that*. I thought I was cleaning and running errands or whatever?"

"You are." His tone was reassuring.

"In *that*?"

"Well, yes. Of course," he replied calmly, adding a soothing lilt to his words and lowering the pitch of his voice just slightly. "All the house staff boys wear this, or a version of it. This one I picked out especially for you." He had been slowly making his way from behind his desk to Nikki's side. "I think if you try it, you'll find the weight quite satisfying." Nikki stared at him and he continued speaking softly, gently, in a practiced, hypnotic tone. "Why don't you just try it on, Nikki? If you really don't care for it, perhaps we can work something else out." He rested one hand lightly on the boy's bare shoulder, practically whispering now. "Go on. Just try it."

Nikki was silent. This was the moment.

"Brian, the mirror." There may have been a touch more urgency in his voice than he'd intended.

Brian set the toolbox on the floor and hurried over to pull a heavy curtain back from an oversized dressing mirror. It was seven feet tall and four feet wide and its heavy, wooden frame was anchored to the wall in several places. Bradford slipped his fingers through the shoulders of the chest harness, taking it from Liam, and coaxed Nikki over to the mirror.

"Look." He slipped his arms around Nikki's shoulders and held the harness up to the boy's chest, whispering in the boy's ear. "You see? Stunning." He kept talking, his voice low and musical, and he kept his lips close to Nikki's ear. "The leather won't bind. It's padded under the shoulder pieces. Liam makes these himself in his shop, and all by hand—he does amazing work. Sometime, I will take you over to see, if you like..." He let his voice trail off.

Nikki stood there, looking in the mirror at himself and at the harness for a long time. Long enough that Bradford was starting to get nervous. This step was crucial to his plans; it was imperative that the boy accept the trappings of the lifestyle if Nikki was going to continue to work at the club.

And Nikki must continue if Bradford had any hope of teaching him everything he wanted to.

"Try it," Bradford whispered once more in Nikki's ear. He felt Nikki sway just the tiniest bit toward his voice, and he smiled slightly but kept a tight lid on his emotions.

"Okay."

Liam stepped forward to help with the buckles, but Bradford stopped him with a quick gesture and settled the harness onto Nikki's shoulders himself. He moved slowly, taking his time gently adjusting and fastening each buckle, keeping close contact with Nikki by sliding his fingers over the boy's skin as he moved from front to back. When he was done, he walked a slow circle around Nikki, then nodded to Liam.

"Nikki, dear, I'm going to let the expert in here to make sure this all fits properly. Are you okay?"

Nikki nodded wordlessly, staring at himself in the mirror.

There was an eruption of pure joy deep in the pit of his soul. Bradford reached out to steady himself, placing one hand on the solid reassurance of the mirror's heavy frame as a bolt of pride traveled up the length of his spine, and another, stronger and darker in nature, drove straight into his groin.

Oh, yes, he thought. *The boy is perfect.*
Perfect.

6

One of the beautiful things about the harness Bradford had picked out for Nikki was that Nikki couldn't completely put it on himself. There was a buckle between Nikki's shoulder blades that absolutely had to be done by a second set of hands. He answered the knock on his bedroom door with anticipation and as Nikki stepped into his room, he gave himself a mental pat on the back, whispering, "Attaboy."

"What?"

"Sorry, nothing," he lied. "Let me have a look." He turned the boy around and fussed with the buckle for a moment. "How does that feel?"

"Fine, I guess."

"Now, you're sure you're all right wearing this?" he asked slyly, as he checked and tested each of the other buckles on the harness, which was absolutely unnecessary.

Bradford noted with amusement that the boy hadn't complained even once about the black leather boy shorts he'd been required to wear with the harness.

"Well, yeah. I mean, if it's the uniform, then what choice

do I have?" Nikki replied with a tone of resignation. Bradford didn't buy it, and he was very pleased about that.

"Indeed." Reluctantly, he forced himself to remove his fingers from the leather and step away from Nikki. "Run along now. You won't want to keep Levi waiting."

"Right."

"Eat something before you head out."

"Will do."

Will do, sir. Bradford mentally corrected the boy, grinning to himself.

Soon.

In the meantime, Bradford needed to clear his evening schedule and prepare himself for the conversation he knew would be coming after Nikki experienced his first day cleaning and restocking the playrooms. It would be an interesting day.

———

Nikki finished off his apple and made his way down the long hall and through the heavy door into the main dining room. At one end of the room, a couple of other guys were waiting; Brian and someone else he didn't recognize were similarly dressed in harnesses and speaking with a third man, who spotted him instantly and waved him over.

"Come join us, Nikki."

He hurried over, falling in line beside Brian.

"Good morning, and welcome. I'm Levi."

Levi was wearing leather pants, a sleeveless white button-down shirt that was open enough to show off his smooth chest, and a collar made of heavy, studded black leather. The collar had a round ring hanging from it and from that, a silver key hung at Levi's throat.

He nodded. "Hey." He shook Levi's hand and looked over at the guy he hadn't met before. "Nikki."

"Jamison. Nice to meet you."

"And you know Brian, of course. You'll be shadowing him today; then you and I will have a chat toward the end of the shift. Your actual shift will be midday, two to eight p.m. You'll have a thirty-minute break to be taken at your discretion. The days will vary week to week as I make the schedules."

"Sounds good."

"Sir," Liam replied.

"Hm?"

"Sounds good, *sir*. I'm not a Master, but I am your supervisor and that is the way we address our superiors out here in the house. I know the kitchen is far less formal, but our members expect a certain level of respect."

"Uh, okay."

Levi raised an eyebrow at him. He blinked for a moment before he got it. "Oh! Okay, *sir*. Sorry."

Brian leaned over, grinning at him. "Sorry, *sir*."

"Wow. Really?" Nikki cleared his throat and tried again. "Okay, sir. Sorry, sir."

Levi laughed. "Very nice. You'll get used to it. You'll hear it all over the house; it will become second nature, I assure you."

He wondered about that, but he nodded anyway.

"You'll generally find me at the bar. I supervise the club during business hours for Master Bradford, and as I need to be readily available to everyone, I use the bar as my office. From there I can deal with the phone, the door, and staff can easily find me."

Nikki nodded again. He didn't dare speak; he was afraid to say the wrong thing.

Levi smiled at him. "Good. Jamison, you'll take three. Brian, second floor, please."

"Yes, sir!" Brian and Jamison answered in unison.

Levi waved them off. "Oh, Brian. Do stick to the second floor today, hm? Master Bradford was very clear that Nikki should steer clear of the third floor for now. He doesn't want to overwhelm the boy on his first day. Start with the light bondage rooms, take your time, and be sure to answer all of Nikki's questions completely. Don't worry if it slows you down; I'll have second shift cover anything you don't get to."

"Yes, sir. Thank you, sir. Come on, Nikki."

He hurried after Brian, who left the dining room and headed straight for the stairs. He was a little confused. He was pretty sure he'd just heard Levi say "bondage room," but he didn't want to ask and make a fool of himself, so he held on to his questions for now.

Nikki noted as they walked that Brian's uniform was different than his own: it was made of softer, wider leather straps that hugged his body and moved with Brian's skin. It crisscrossed in a complicated pattern across his entire torso, and it had a ring in the back as well as in front.

Brian reached for a key that hung on a strap at his hip and opened up the very first door they came to. "Each of the rooms at the club is a little different. This one is the simplest and can serve a lot of different purposes. Some of the rooms farther down the hall have more tailored uses. And the rooms on the third floor are very specific."

The third floor that Bradford didn't want him to see today. What the hell was on the third floor?

He followed Brian inside and had a look around, more than a little shocked to realize that Levi really had said "bondage room." He also sensed, as soon as the door closed behind them, that the room was soundproofed. "Oh, my God."

"Nice, right?"

The floor under his feet was black and made of a nonslip material that looked like rubber. He figured it must have padding underneath of some kind, because it gave a little under his feet. Two of the walls in the room were covered in heavy red curtains and the third, opposite the door, was black and had a set of chains attached to it by heavy metal rings. Next to the chains on the wall hung a clear-fronted cabinet full of a variety of cuffs in different sizes and colors: padded, fur-lined, stiff leather, a set with studs on the outside, and another set with something rough and studded on the inside. There was a large, iron-framed bed set up against one of the curtained walls; it was made up with a dark red comforter, and the frame was painted matte black. The headboard was nearly obscured by a ton of pillows.

He turned toward Brian, his heart pounding slightly. "What is this place?"

Brian was across the room, hanging what looked like a riding crop on a hook on the far wall. Nikki stared, eyes going wide as he caught sight of all the other things hanging there: whips in a bunch of sizes, a variety of paddles, long and short crops, long strips of leather.

"Brian?"

Brian smiled at him, speaking softly. "It's a bondage room, Nikki. Have you never seen one?"

"No, Brian. Not the room. What is *this place*? This building. What goes on here?" When he'd started in the kitchen, he'd thought it was a restaurant and bar. After a while he'd figured out that it was some kind of members-only club for men. Nikki realized when he saw himself in the mirror, wearing Bradford's hand-chosen uniform, that there was something kinky going on, but even then he'd figured it was like a Hooters vibe or a Tilted Kilt. Sexy waitstaff, that kind of thing.

"Ohhhh. Oh, my." Brian walked over, took him by the shoulders, and led him over to the bed. "Sit."

Nikki was fighting the urge to run. He felt it building in his body, that flight response he got when things just felt *off*. Like when someone came into an alley he was sleeping in. Like when a couple of guys crossed the street toward him or when a cop flashed a badge. But Brian's hands were warm on his shoulders, and nothing about the last couple of months was telling him he was unsafe. It was just that all this added up to something much...bigger...and more intimidating than he'd expected.

"It's a dungeon, isn't it?" He'd heard stories on the street.

"No. It's a gentlemen's club."

"For BDSM."

"Yes. That is practiced here in a safe environment. It's also a social club."

"Social?"

"Sure, for the club's members. Masters, submissives, some with ties or contracts and some without. There are parties and events, the dining room, the bar."

Everything was moving in slow motion in Nikki's mind, but pieces of a much larger puzzle started coming together, falling into place. "Bradford is a Dom."

"Yes. And I am a submissive."

"For him?"

"Sometimes."

He looked at Brian sharply. "By choice?"

"*Of course.*" Brian looked horrified. "Oh, my God. All by choice. You have to pay to be a member, Dom, or sub. You're interviewed, background checked. You don't get to come here unless you're experienced, and Master Bradford is convinced it's what you want. What you *really* want. It's not easy to get in."

He nodded slowly. "And that's why you—why everyone —calls him Master Bradford."

"It's his club. He's the owner, the head Master. Everyone defers to him, even the other Doms."

"I don't." He hadn't been deferring to anyone. He wasn't experienced, wasn't paying any dues.

"Master Bradford told me you're an employee. You're not a sub, you're not a member, you don't need to call him Master. You just work here."

He nodded. He just worked at the club. It was a job, and a well-paying one at that. *Suck it up,* he told himself. *It's weird and kinky, but it's just a job.*

He sighed. "Sorry. I just...didn't know."

"That's the thing about this place. You're not going to know anything unless you ask."

That was for damn sure.

"Are you okay?"

"Sure. Yes." He stood up. "Let's get back to work." He could feel Brian's eyes on him, but Brian didn't argue.

"Okay." Brian headed over to a chest by the bathroom door and opened it, pulling out two sets of latex gloves. "Everything in that chest has been sterilized, so we don't want to touch any of it with our bare hands." Brian pulled on his gloves and headed into the bathroom where he opened up a portable dishwasher sitting on top of the counter. "Ooh. Good choices." Brian pulled out a couple of items that sent Nikki's imagination into a wild tailspin. All he could think was, *Ouch.* "Gloves on, please."

He raised an eyebrow but pulled them on.

"Glass dildo. That's a nice one. Good heft and not so long you feel like you swallowed it." Brian put the toy into his hands. "A couple of silicone cock rings, and this is a beaded anal probe. Someone had a good time last night." Brian laughed and closed the dishwasher, then stepped around him. "Come on."

He followed Brian back to the big chest with his hands full and his eyes wide. He knew he must look ridiculous, but Brian was completely relaxed about it. "These go in the drawers. It's pretty easy; everything has a place so you can usually tell what's missing. Butt plugs and anal toys in this drawer, the glass dildos go in that one, and the rings are up here." Brian casually put everything away, taking the toys one by one from his fingers.

"For cleaning, we deal with toys, instruments like the crops and paddles, towels, a few of the smaller benches, and all the soft goods like pillows and bedding. The overnight custodians handle the floors, the bathrooms, and the big furniture. Master Bradford also has a special crew come in twice a week to care for and treat all the leather on everything, so we just have to point out the things that need work, and they take care of them. Levi keeps a list—call down any time you find something, and he'll add it. If something is broken or worn beyond repair, or you think it's not getting clean, bring it to Levi too."

So...wait.

There were actual crews in this city that you could hire to take care of leather weapons and bondage gear? There were custodians that came in and scrubbed sweat and come off the floors and lube out of the bathtub? People really did this shit for a living?

Nikki blinked. Well, if people could do *that* to put food on their tables and pay their rent, then he could handle this, right? It didn't mean he had to be into the scene. It didn't mean he was anyone's sub. It was a paycheck.

Right?

Right.

It was a job. And by the way, who exactly was he worried about embarrassing himself in front of anyway? He had no family anymore—well, none that cared about him—and he was finally making some friends here. And frankly, a rent-free roof over his head, three squares a day, and a steady paycheck made this gig a no-brainer. The last time he could count on regular meals and a roof over his head, he was about nine years old. After that it was his dad's van, his mom's friend's house, one shelter after another, and finally the street.

Who was he to judge?

"You okay?"

Nikki blinked at Brian. "Oh. Yeah, I'm sorry, I was thinking."

"It's a great place to work, Nikki. I'm telling you. Master Bradford will always treat you with respect."

Nikki nodded. "I'm good. Show me how to clean the leather."

The next couple of hours kept them busy. Nikki did his best to throw himself into the work and to make sure Brian's time with him wasn't wasted. He learned about the different first aid ointments and creams and other items stocked in the first aid kits in each of the rooms. He learned what several of the tools and instruments were and how they were used. He learned about Bradford's video surveillance system and that Bradford hired both subs and Doms as security to monitor the activities in each room in real time. He touched chains and cuffs. He asked Brian dozens of questions.

By the time their lunch break came around, Nikki felt pretty relaxed. He could do this. This was easy. A little weird...but easy.

"How is the student, Brian?" Levi came over and joined them at their table while they ate.

Brian's mouth was full and he quickly swallowed down his bite of salad. "He's a natural, sir."

"Really?" Levi looked pleased. "So glad to hear it. You think you're a natural, Nikki?"

"Well, it is pretty straightforward."

"Sir," Levi corrected, but he didn't wait for Nikki to repeat himself. He just nodded. "It is straightforward. And you're comfortable with the equipment?"

"Well, it's nothing I've been exposed to before, so it was a bit..."

"Intimidating?"

"At first, yes."

"Sir."

He shook his head. "Yes, sir."

"And now?"

"Well? It's not like anything is going to jump out and bite me." *Oh, shit.* His eyes popped open wide as he remembered this time. "Uh...jump out and bite me, *sir.*"

Levi laughed. "No, those things are locked up on the third floor."

Nikki stopped just short of taking a bite of his cheeseburger.

Levi laughed. "I'm kidding. Although the third floor is a lot more intense. You'll be ready for that eventually, and if not, that's fine. The other boys on your shift are."

Nikki nodded. Whatever it was, he figured he could handle it.

Levi looked between them. "You can always tell a sub

that has evening plans. He'll be the one eating like a bird. Eh, Brian?"

Brian blushed. "Yes, sir."

"Who with tonight?"

"I accepted an invitation from Master Richard, sir."

"Oh, very nice. I've worked with him. What are your plans? Ropes, I assume?"

"Yes, sir. He wants to practice his knots. And he promised me a spanking." Brian grinned.

Levi laughed. "And so, a salad."

Nikki snorted. Barely two months ago he was so hungry, he almost gave a guy a blowjob for a cheeseburger. He thought better of it and went hungry that day. If there was a burger to be had for free, though, he was going for it.

For free, not for a spanking.

"I'm not a sub."

Levi nodded. "Sir."

"I'm not a sub, sir."

"Mm." He wasn't sure what Levi's look meant. "Master Bradford did tell me that. That's interesting." Levi stood up again. "Enjoy that cheeseburger."

"Yes, sir."

Interesting?

Levi left them, heading for his office behind the bar.

———

Nikki's afternoon was a little more intense. The rooms at the end of the hall had bondage furniture the likes of which he'd never heard of, let alone seen: crosses and cages and stockades, bondage horses and suspension contraptions. Things that Brian explained with enthusiasm, leaving Nikki nearly speechless. He listened, but he wasn't sure he really understood.

He headed back to his room before dinner and took a long, thoughtful shower. When he got out, he was pretty much ready to relax and watch some TV, but he found a note on his bed:

I would be delighted if you would be my guest this evening for dinner in the main dining room at seven.

Warmly, Bradford.

It was handwritten in such ornate cursive, he had to read it again to be sure he'd gotten it right.

Delighted? Did real people even talk like that? Nikki had no idea how to interpret the invitation, but he wasn't going to say no to dinner. Especially since Bradford had been good to him and hadn't asked for anything in return except that he do the job he was being paid for. Bradford was kind of cool, too, like after the whole homeless thing. He seemed like a good guy, even if his club was...whatever it was.

Nikki dug around in the closet and the drawers of his dresser and came up with khakis and a soft blue sweater, figuring an invitation to dinner in the formal dining room meant he should wear something nicer than his jeans. He probably should wear a tie too, but he didn't have one.

He lay the clothing out on his bed and went into the bathroom to fix his hair. He shaved even though he really didn't need to; it was a good thing he didn't care for facial hair since he had little hope of ever growing a beard.

He'd forgotten that he left his harness hanging there on a towel rack before his shower and he reached for it, shaking his head at himself. He'd actually had to call Levi to undo the buckle at the back so he could get it off. God, that was so embarrassing. Next time he'd remember to ask someone when his shift ended.

He ran his fingers over the leather. Brian looked good in his uniform; the guy obviously liked it and wore it like a second skin. He wondered if he'd ever be as unapologetically himself as Brian. He figured that required *knowing* who you were first, and Nikki knew he wasn't there yet. He'd spent far too much time just surviving to have figured that out. It had never mattered—who he was came down to trying to get homework done while he was broke, hungry, and homeless.

These days? Well, sometimes he was at loose ends. What did people do with time on their hands?

Apparently, they had dinner together.

He shrugged and grabbed the harness as he left the bathroom, dug the special hanger Liam had given him for it out of his closet, and hung it up.

7

B radford made his way past the bar and gave Joseph a nod. "Good evening."

"Evening, sir."

Joe was a civilian, but he was a damn good bartender. He was also classically handsome, had that ubiquitous thirtysomething look, and he loved men. He was flirty but unavailable, and as far as Bradford was concerned, that was the perfect formula for keeping an unoccupied Dom at the bar. He also had great taste in music, and right now he was playing Bill Withers and grooving as he cleaned glasses and looked over his stock. Nothing like a little soul to put you in the mood.

Speaking of moods, it was time to go check on his sub for the evening. He'd left the boy to some quiet contemplation in his office after a successful workday, and he had every intention of rewarding the boy for his effort. He felt his steps grow lighter as he returned and went inside, closing the door loudly behind him, testing how deep the boy had gone while he was away.

Levi didn't even twitch.

Bradford looked the boy over. He'd left Levi on his knees, bent forward with his forehead on the floor, ass in the air, and his hands resting, crossed and palms up, on his lower back. One of Bradford's favorite ways to immobilize his subs without restraints.

He walked over and drew a finger along the waistband of Levi's leather shorts. "How do you feel, boy?"

The answer came slowly, and Bradford was patient as Levi pulled himself from deep subspace to reply. "Relaxed, sir. My fingers are just beginning to get a bit tingly."

"Ah. Thank you, boy." Levi's honesty spoke of experience. Brian would have allowed his fingers to go completely numb before he said anything—and had. "I was just going to ask you to make your way to your feet anyway. Do you require assistance?"

"No, sir. Just a moment if it pleases you, sir."

"The moment is yours, boy. Take your time." Bradford made his way over to his desk to give Levi more room and less scrutiny.

Levi was practically an artist; his particular brand of submission was a noble pursuit, bringing a kind of regal dignity and gracefulness to everything he did. Technically perfect, his joy was in serving and only light bondage. He had no love for a whip or a paddle, no tolerance or need for real pain, but you wouldn't find a sub more creative and dedicated to his service anywhere. Bradford had nothing but respect for him.

Levi was also an absolute animal in bed. A consummate bottom, but the most demanding goddamn fuck he'd ever been with.

Levi rocked back on his heels and unfolded slowly, eyes studiously low as he stood, settling easily into the display pose he knew Bradford preferred. Levi served many Masters at the club, Bradford being one of particular tastes, and Levi seemed only too happy to please.

"Ready, sir."

He moved toward Levi and walked an agonizingly slow circle around the boy. It was hardly necessary, but he knew Levi got off on a careful inspection, and this evening was a reward, after all. He admired the pride Levi took in his service: chin high and eyes low. Bradford took a moment to smooth and straighten the boy's shorts, indulging himself by slipping his fingers up and under each leg and around the full circle of the boy's waistband. He finished off by firmly gripping the bulge in Levi's tight leather shorts.

Levi offered him a lovely sigh.

"I want this cock hard for me before we get to the dining room, boy."

"Yes, sir. My pleasure, sir." The boy would be hard before they left his office.

"Our usual rules and customs, hm? Do you need a reminder?"

"No, sir."

Of course not.

"Door."

Levi stepped around him and pulled open the office door.

"At heel, in step."

"As it pleases you, Master."

He allowed himself a smile. It did please him, in fact. He stepped through the door and felt Levi fall in dutifully behind him. He didn't give the boy another thought as he entered the main part of the club, passing once more by the bar. He glanced at his watch.

"Sir," Joe greeted him as he made his way by. Bradford inclined his head but said nothing.

He did, however, greet numerous members, Doms and subs alike, as he made his way through the long bar and lounge area and headed toward the dining room. When he finally arrived, the evening's host, a muscular, red-haired sub named Andrew, greeted him with a smile and a bow. "Good evening, sir."

"Good evening, Andrew," Bradford answered smoothly, noting the degree of confidence in Andrew's voice. Mentally he made a note that should he ever need an evening off, the combination of Andrew, Joe, and Levi as a team, supervised peripherally by nearly any Dom, could surely cover for his absence.

Good to know.

"If it pleases you, sir, may I confirm that you have not requested your usual table but the small table in the west corner?"

"Yes. Thank you, Andrew. That is correct." He required more privacy tonight than his usual table right in the middle of the dining room could afford him, a more discreet environment for his conversation. This would be another pivotal evening in his grand plan for Nikki, and he didn't want distractions or interruptions.

"Excellent. We have your table ready as you requested, sir." Andrew led the way and Bradford followed.

"You will instruct the staff that Levi will be serving us this evening. They need only bring drinks and food as ordered; it will be Levi's privilege."

"Very good, sir. I will let Timothy know."

"Thank you, boy."

Levi moved quickly to his chair and pulled it out for him. Once he was seated, Levi pulled out his napkin and placed it in his lap and filled his water glass as well. The boy then took his place, not kneeling but standing several steps behind Bradford's chair. Bradford picked up his water glass and glanced at his watch again. He was right on time.

Nikki wasn't.

Oh, the punishments he could dream up for a naughty boy who was perpetually late. He swallowed and forced that image away. For the moment, Nikki was still—*still, dammit*—just an employee. But with any luck, Brian's enthusiasm had been somewhat influential today and Nikki was at least curious. Bradford was counting on it, and in moments, he would know.

Assuming Nikki showed up.

With his usual arrogance, he realized that he'd failed to consider the possibility that the boy wasn't interested in dinner with him. But just as that unsettling thought settled over him, Nikki appeared in the doorway leading to his neighboring brownstone and surveyed the room.

"Go and fetch him, boy."

"Yes, sir."

Levi hurried toward Nikki, long legs taking little time to close the gap between them. They had a quick exchange of words before Levi led Nikki back to the table.

Bradford stood as the boys arrived. "Good evening, Nikki. Thank you for joining me."

Levi went straight to Nikki's chair and pulled it out for him. "No problem. I was hungry...oh. Thanks, Levi."

"My pleasure, sir."

"Well, I'm not...uh. I mean..." Bradford watched Nikki blink at Levi as he sat down and Levi repeated his earlier ritual, placing Nikki's napkin in his lap and filling his water glass. Levi then repeated the entire scenario once more for Bradford.

"Thank you, boy." Bradford couldn't stop himself from

acknowledging Levi's status in front of Nikki, just to see how Nikki reacted.

"It is my pleasure to serve, Master Bradford."

Oh, Levi was at his most formal tonight. The boy must be feeling the need to impress Nikki. How wonderful.

"Have a look at the menu."

"Oh, right. Sure."

"I recommend the braised lamb chops if you're in the mood for something substantial. The fish is much lighter. Both are typically excellent." Chef Reggie was quite a find. Though a consummate sub himself, with Bradford's blessing, Reggie had full command of the club's kitchen.

"I was actually looking at the lasagna."

Bradford smiled. "Whatever suits you."

Nikki nodded. "Yeah. Lasagna."

Timothy arrived at their table seconds later and knelt near his chair, and Bradford shook his head. "Up, boy." Bradford was well aware that Timothy was still training in the dining room. "While I appreciate the respect, boy, you needn't kneel when you are working. Keep your eyes low and simply greet me as you would anyone else at the club, hm?"

"Yes, sir. I'm sorry, sir."

"That's quite all right, Timothy."

There was a moment of silence. Levi finally cleared his throat.

"Oh! Um. Good evening, sir. What can I get for you this evening?"

He smiled. "Very nice, Timothy. I will have the lamb chops. Ask Chef for rice instead of potatoes; he won't be surprised. And a glass of whatever wine Chef recommends to pair with it."

"Yes, sir. And your..." Timothy looked at Nikki.

"Guest," he prompted.

"Your guest, sir?"

Nikki raised an eyebrow. "The lasagna, please, and a Coke."

Timothy nodded. "Anything for your boy, sir?"

"No, thank you, Timothy. Levi prefers not to eat while he is serving. An extra glass of water will do."

"Yes, sir. Right away, sir." Timothy turned and practically ran back to the kitchen.

He laughed. "Tim is new to the dining room. He once served in the house, as you are now. He's very polite and respectful. He's going to do very well."

"I haven't met him yet. And Levi is...you're his Dom?"

"We've an agreement for this evening."

"Huh."

"You look nice. Handsome." Adorable. Delicious.

"Oh, thanks. I didn't have a tie..."

"No matter, we see all manner of dress in the dining room depending on what various members have planned. You look just fine."

Nikki smiled at him, shyly, and it was all Bradford could do to keep his itchy fingers in his lap. "Thank you."

"Tell me how your first day went."

Nikki laughed. "Oh, God."

Timothy came back with a tray and held it while Levi served drinks and set a basket of bread on the table in front of Nikki.

"You'll have to tell me what that means."

"Oh. Well, it was fine. I just...I was a little out of my league."

"Nonsense. I believe you are fully capable of the required duties," he replied, knowing very well that wasn't what Nikki was talking about.

"No, no. That's not what I mean." Nikki picked up his Coke and sipped it. "I just...I honestly didn't know what this club was about."

"Oh, I see. You weren't aware that I operate a BDSM establishment?"

Nikki snorted and rolled his eyes. "No, I wasn't *aware* that you *operate a BDSM establishment*. I was not *aware* at all."

Bradford raised an eyebrow, though he hadn't intended it to climb all the way into his hairline. "You're...mocking me?"

"Well, you do sometimes talk like you have a rod up your ass, Bradford."

Levi coughed behind him.

Bradford could hardly blame the boy; it was all he could do not to stand up and put Nikki in his place himself. He opened his mouth and closed it again, biting his lips together. Oh, when he finally got what he wanted, he was so looking forward to keeping that smart ass rosy.

Did you hear that, love? Does the boy remind you of anyone? Harrison would have laughed himself sick....Bradford still missed that laugh.

After a moment's pause and a very deep breath, he tried again. "Yes, well. Others have expressed similar sentiments in the past." Usually Tobias or Luca, though typically not while sober.

"Seriously, can you hear yourself talk?" Nikki laughed. "Anyway, Brian had to do a lot of explaining."

"I'm sure. And what is your impression?"

"My impression?"

Oh, for the love of— "What did you think, Nikki?"

"Oh. Well, I'm not a sub, so..."

"So you can't have an opinion?"

"Of course I have an opinion."

"Oh? Excellent. Which was your favorite room?" Bradford asked carefully.

"My...uh..."

Bradford watched the wheels turn as Nikki tried to sort through the implications of the question. Phrasing his inquiry in such a way as to assume Nikki *had* a favorite should force a positive response.

"Well, the room with the big cross was pretty cool."

Oh.

Oh, good Lord in Heaven, he was going to implode. There were at least six rooms on the second floor that were less intense than the St. Andrews room. That room was meant to be intimidating, the big cross dominating the space, built and braced in the center of the room instead of against a wall as was typical. And yet...the boy went straight for it.

"Oh? Why is that?"

Would you like to try it? Can I take you upstairs right now? Oh, the things I could do to you, Nikki. I could make you love it. I could make you scream. I know I could. It could be so good, my boy.

"...so that was cool."

He swallowed and blinked at Nikki. "I'm sorry, I...say again?" Christ, it was quite possible he could not be trusted alone with this boy.

Ever.

"Oh, just that the cross is so cool and imposing in that room and the leather and mahogany work and all the studs are so ornate. Also, the cuffs hanging from the ceiling at the other end of the room? Whoa."

That was the other bondage element in the room, and

those cuffs hung on very heavy chains and came straight down from the ceiling. "They're height adjustable."

Nikki nodded and Bradford noted with no small delight the blush in the boy's cheeks.

He pounced. "You're curious," he said deliberately. Not a question, but a statement that required a response.

"Oh. Oh, well, I don't know. I'm really...I mean I don't know anything about...uh." Nikki picked up his Coke and sipped it.

The boy didn't say no. He absolutely did not say no. Bradford seized on the moment as he had in his study the day Nikki was fitted for his uniform. He leaned forward, bracing one forearm in front of him on the table. "Well, of course not. I understand it can be strange and...confusing."

"Confusing?" Nikki's sapphire eyes locked on to his, melting him a little.

"Of course. It's hard to know exactly how you feel about it, right? I'm sure it seems intimidating. Perhaps it may even seem scary. And yet perhaps, at the same time, it might be something you'd like to learn more about. Possibly even try one day, hm?"

"Oh, I..."

"I mean, how would you know?" His voice deepened into a seductive purr, the words slipping from his lips smoothly. "How *could* you possibly know unless you tried it. With someone you trust, of course. Someone you know has your well-being at heart. Someone who believes in you."

Someone like me. Someone who can teach you how to fly.

"With someone I trust. Maybe."

Bradford let the tentative agreement hang between them for a long breath and allowed the hypnotic moment to dissolve on its own. Then he slowly picked up his wine and leaned back in his chair, crossing one leg over the other. "I'd be happy to take you up and let you try some of the equipment out sometime, just to see what it's like." He casually sipped his wine, not knowing exactly what to expect in answer. But it was no matter. The boy was curious now, and that was all it took. It was only a matter of time.

Patience, He reminded himself. That word was becoming his mantra.

"Oh, well. I don't know."

He waved a hand, dismissing Nikki's concerns. "Not to worry. The offer stands if you're ever interested."

If he didn't know better, he'd swear Chef timed their meals perfectly to punctuate the end to their conversation. Levi sprang into action, serving them and refilling water glasses and his wine.

He noticed the way Nikki was watching Levi, and once the boy had completed his tasks and returned to his place, Nikki leaned closer. "He works here. I mean, today he was my boss."

"And he will be again tomorrow."

"But now he's...?"

"Ah. Levi is employed here as my daytime manager, Nikki. But Levi is also a submissive and a member of the club. Tonight he is choosing to serve. He and I made arrangements earlier in the week. It's a mere coincidence that the boy I've contracted with for the evening happens to also be your supervisor."

In fact, it wasn't much of a coincidence at all, but Nikki didn't need to know that.

"So he's not working."

"Oh, no. The boy is not in my employment just now. He is my sub."

"Because...he wants to?"

"Levi?"

Levi stepped forward. "How may I be of service, sir?"

"Are you in my service this evening because you choose to be, or because you are obligated to be?"

"It is of my own free will that I serve you this evening, and it is my honor, sir."

"Thank you, boy. But now that you have agreed to serve me, what of that free will?"

Levi slipped gracefully but quickly to his knees. "I have no will that is not your own, Master. I am yours."

"Just so. Very good, boy."

He reached out and ran his fingers through Levi's hair, smiled at Nikki, and held up his wineglass. "Well, then. To new experiences."

Nikki was silent but picked up his glass and politely touched it to Bradford's before taking a sip.

"Let's eat while this delightful meal is still hot, shall we?"

8

Bradford wasn't able to sleep a wink that night, despite several intense and energetic attempts by Levi to wear him out. Dawn arrived in all its bright and shining glory without him having closed his eyes for more than a moment.

He rolled over and hit the Call button on his nightstand, and Jamison appeared instantly and silently in his doorway.

Coffee, Bradford mouthed at him. Jamison nodded and disappeared.

He reached a hand out for Levi's solid warmth, running his fingers over the boy's bare shoulders and down his spine to his lower back. Levi sighed softly.

"Shh. Just saying good morning, boy. Nothing more." He was fairly sure Levi would have quite a time walking today after their acrobatics the night before, but really, that was just an excuse. He didn't have it in him this morning, either.

"Your hands are warm, sir."

"Yes, well. You are a furnace in your sleep, my boy."

Levi laughed and rolled over, but the boy's face fell when he got a good look at him. Bradford permitted the boy eye contact in bed, and Levi wasn't shy about telling Bradford what he saw. "Are you well, sir?"

"I'm fine, boy."

"With all due respect, sir, you don't appear to have slept."

"Mmm. No. I have not."

"My apologies, sir, if I haven't—"

He laid a finger over Levi's lips and mustered a tired smile. "You have. I have something on my mind is all."

Levi sighed. "How may I serve you, sir?"

There was a soft knock at the door, and Jamison came in with a tray.

"Ah. Thank you, boy."

"My pleasure, sir." Jamison set the tray down on the dresser, then hurried out of the room.

"You can start with the coffee, I suppose."

Levi slipped out of bed and poured two mugs of coffee, leaving Bradford's black but adding cream and sugar to his own. Bradford accepted a mug and sipped deeply.

"What is your impression of Nikki, Levi?"

"He seems to have settled in quickly, sir."

"Mm. Yes. But what do you *think* of him?"

"Sir?" Levi looked at him.

"You know what I am asking, Levi. Speak frankly and we'll keep this conversation between us, hm? Do you think he's suited to our lifestyle?"

"He's young, but I think he is perfectly suited, sir. Brian said he was full of curiosity and interest as they worked yesterday. He said that Nikki was asking him personal questions as well, about why he subbed, how and when he knew what he wanted."

Wasn't that delicious?

He shook his head. "I have such high hopes for the boy, Levi. He took to that sub's harness like he was born for it. He put it on yesterday with a pride I don't think he understands yet. And you had to see him looking at himself in the mirror the day Liam and I fitted him. It was like he finally recognized the person looking back at him. It was breathtaking."

"That's incredible."

"It is. So much potential."

So much responsibility.

"I do think he could be easily overwhelmed, sir."

"Oh, yes." Levi had hit on it exactly. "That's been my fear all along. I've got to take things slowly." He looked at Levi. "He isn't to go anywhere near that third floor, Levi. Not for anything. Not yet." That could derail everything.

"Yes, sir. I will see to it, sir."

Bradford nodded. The third floor boasted the club's specialized and fetish rooms: the White Room, the Heavy Bondage Room, the Sensory Deprivation Room (also known as the Black Room), the Torture Chamber. The room Bradford's predecessor had installed to suit his own desires was on the third floor as well; he'd referred to that room as the Lab, and every surface including the ceiling was covered in ceramic tile. Each of those rooms could be, and were essentially intended to be, daunting for even the club's most experienced players. There were several Doms and many subs who had never seen the inside of those rooms at all.

It was impossible to say at this point how far Nikki would eventually be willing to go. He had his suspicions, drawing solely from his own experience, but there truly was no way to be sure without taking all the appropriate early steps first.

"Levi."

"Yes, Master?"

"You will tell me if you feel that my judgment is off,

won't you? If it becomes clear that Nikki is stressed or anxious, or that he isn't suited to the lifestyle and I am...only seeing what I want to see?"

Bradford was rarely given to confiding in subs or asking for their advice. Most subs had a hard time compartmentalizing such things, and frankly, it wouldn't be fair of Bradford to ask, given his authority at the club. But Levi was a longtime member, going back nearly as far as Bradford himself, and he had an uncanny knack for reading people. It was part of what made him so good at serving. He was able to anticipate a need, a desire, often before it was clear to the Dom himself.

"Are you asking that of me, sir?"

He sighed and looked at Levi. "I am. I have to ask someone." It ought to be a Dom, but following his predecessor's custom, and in part due to his own arrogance, Bradford was the only full-time Dom that worked at the club.

"It will require honesty that could be construed as disrespect, sir."

"I know it's a lot to ask. I will expect frank words, and there will be no reprimand for your honesty, just gratitude for your counsel."

"Then, yes, sir. I will monitor for you."

"Thank you, Levi. I am very pleased by your willingness to serve."

"It's my honor, Master."

His judgment wasn't off; he was very sure of that. Nikki was perfect. What was off was actually his self-control around the boy, but he couldn't say that to Levi. Nikki's education and training were going to require all of his patience and restraint. He was already light-years ahead of the boy in his own mind. If Nikki began to feel uncomfortable, it would be because he was pushing him too hard or too fast, and Levi would certainly pick up on another sub's distress.

He only wished he could completely trust himself. It had been a long time since he'd groomed a sub, and he'd never been so utterly fascinated—or, to be honest, obsessed —by anyone.

"Would you like me to start a shower for you, sir? Will you allow me to serve you? I'll have to get ready for work shortly thereafter."

And there was Levi, reliably one step ahead of him. "Yes, boy. Thank you."

Levi got out of bed, refilled his coffee, and hurried off to start the shower.

9

"Thank you, boy."

Nikki was leaving his room when he caught sight of Bradford and Levi in the upstairs hall. He froze.

"It's always my honor, Master Bradford. Thank you." Levi dropped to his knees and kissed the toes of each of Bradford's dress shoes in turn, then stood again. His eyes were low, and he was dressed much as he'd been the day before when Nikki showed up for work.

"I look forward to the next opportunity, boy. Move along now, I won't be the reason you're late."

"Yes, sir. Have a good day, sir."

As Levi hurried off, Bradford turned and caught sight of Nikki. "Ah. Good morning, boy. Do you need assistance with your harness?"

"Yes. Please." Nikki made his way over. *Boy?* Part of him bristled at the nickname, but part of him, he was starting to learn, wanted to fit in. Wanted to belong. He'd never really felt like he fit anywhere. Levi was comfortable with the word, and so was Brian. Jamison didn't seem to give it a second thought, either. It was just what Bradford did. He called people "boy."

He felt Bradford step around him, aware of the man's fingers on his shoulders and the fact that Bradford was standing close enough for him to feel warm breath on his neck. Bradford tugged and tightened the buckle, then stepped away.

"There you are. All set."

"Levi stayed the night?" He couldn't help it; he had to ask.

"Yes, Nikki. That was part of our agreement."

"Is he your lover?"

Bradford smiled. "No."

"Do you pay him?"

Bradford raised an eyebrow and straightened his shoulders. "Don't be insulting, Nikki. Levi is no whore, and I am no pimp."

"Oh..." Wow, Bradford sounded pretty pissed.

"We made an arrangement prior to last evening that he would serve me, and I would reward him with an evening of intimacy. We're consenting adults, boy."

"Sorry. I was just asking." How was he supposed to learn this shit if he didn't ask?

"Ah." Bradford sighed and Nikki watched him as he grimaced and rubbed his forehead. "Of course you wouldn't know, would you? I apologize for my temper, Nikki, I didn't sleep well. Contracts, be they for a day or a year, vary in every manner imaginable. Why don't you talk with Levi about it? I'm certain he'd be happy to explain. Run along, now. Be sure to have something to eat before your shift begins."

Well, duh. Of course Bradford didn't sleep; he was fucking Levi all night.

Nikki tried to smooth it over with a quick, "Yes, sir." Bradford still looked a little annoyed, but at least he hadn't completely blown it. He hurried off, stopping by the kitchen.

"Good morning, Nikki!"

He smiled. "Morning, Chef."

"Hungry?"

"Can I grab a muffin?"

"Basket on the table. Grab a juice, too."

"Thanks. How's it going?" He helped himself to a muffin and leaned over the table, stuffing it into his mouth in big bites.

"Fine, fine. You moved up fast. We miss you around here."

He shrugged and swallowed down the muffin with a giant gulp of orange juice.

"Come by and chat sometime, I'll fix you something special."

"Sounds good."

"You look great, by the way."

He looked down at his harness. "Yeah?"

"Yeah. That harness really suits you."

He smiled. "Thanks, Chef. And thanks for the breakfast. Gotta run!"

"Be a good boy!"

He snorted on his way out of the kitchen. He wasn't sure why Chef thought the harness suited him exactly, but he didn't hate it. It was comfortable and it helped him fit in with everybody. It made him feel like he belonged, and everyone complimented him on it.

He was still chewing the last bite of his muffin when he found Jamison and another man he hadn't met yet in the dining room having a conversation.

"Levi was with Master Bradford last night." Jamison said quietly.

"Oh, yeah? Lucky."

"Master Bradford or Levi?"

"Both." The two men laughed.

The other guy was about Levi's height, young also, maybe twenty-five or so, and he had lovely olive-toned skin. He stuck out his hand when he noticed Nikki was standing there.

"Hey, I'm Cade."

"Nikki." Cade had striking green eyes too.

"Good morning, boys."

"Morning, sir." Jamison and Cade answered quickly.

He blinked and stammered, "Uh. Good morning, sir."

Levi nodded to them. "Cade, you'll be training Nikki today. Second floor exclusively, please. Jamison, you'll take the third floor on your own."

"Yes, sir."

"Good. Cade and Nikki, get to work. You know where to find me if you need me. Jamison, come with me for a moment." Nikki couldn't help but notice the little hitch in Levi's gait as he walked away with Jamison at his heels.

"Okay, let's get to it." Cade led the way up the staircase. Nikki wondered at the mirror that ran the entire length of the wall up to the second floor, but he found himself looking at himself in it, admiring the lines of his harness. He kind of thought Chef was right; it did look good on him.

"I expected to see Brian this morning."

"Oh, he's off today. He works pretty much the whole weekend in the dining room."

"Really?"

"Well, he works through the dinner rush until maybe

nine, and then he almost always has a session set up after that. He's popular."

"Wow."

"I know, right? Between working and playing, he's here almost as much as Master Bradford is."

Brian did seem enthusiastic about the place yesterday. "Where are we starting?"

"I like to work my way forward. Start with the big rooms first."

"Sure, okay." He followed Cade down the hall.

"How goes it so far?"

"Fine."

Cade keyed into the largest room, the one with the big cross. The minute Nikki walked into the room, he got the same feeling he'd had the day before. It was beautiful, for sure, and seeing the cuffs and shackles attached to it made his pulse race a little.

"Nice, right?"

He nodded. "It's beautiful workmanship."

"It's called a St. Andrew's Cross. Master Bradford had this one made custom for the height of this room. Usually they're up against a wall, you know? But this one just looks like it's floating out here in the middle of nowhere."

"Yeah." Nikki didn't understand what he was feeling or what it meant—he just knew this curious piece of furniture was calling to him somehow.

"You ask for it a lot?"

"Ask...oh." He laughed, feeling a little nervous for some reason. "No. I'm not a...I haven't. I've never—"

"Never?"

He looked at Cade. "No?"

Cade grinned at him. "Well, come on, then."

"What?"

"You wanna try it out?"

"Oh. I don't know..." But his feet were moving.

"It's not a big deal. You won't get in trouble for just trying it. We just can't do up the cuffs or anything without security freaking out." Cade guided him right up to it, turning him to face it. "Stretch your arms out...yeah, up like that. Just hold on to the cuffs to get the idea. And spread out your legs."

His heart started to thud in his chest, and he swallowed.

"Wider. Yeah, like that."

"Wow."

"Got you going, huh?" Cade laughed.

"Maybe?" *Not maybe. Yes.* He watched Cade walk a circle around the cross. They met eyes between the arms of the enormous X as the guy moved in front; then he felt the other boy's eyes on his back as Cade disappeared behind him again.

"You should make sure your Dom knows."

"Uh. Right." His palms were starting to sweat, and he stepped away from the cross abruptly.

"I come up here sometimes with Master Ryan. He's a heavy hitter. He likes long, sustained scenes with a lot of flogging, so he uses the wider fronds and he can just go forever. Takes me right out of my head, you know? I just...float off. It's amazing."

"Do you let him fuck you?"

"Master Ryan?" Cade shook his head. "No, that's not what our sessions are about. I mean, sometimes he strokes off after he gets a good look at his work, and once or twice he's taken me that far accidentally, but that's not the goal, and actual sex isn't ever in our agreement."

"So you don't have to have sex?"

Cade snorted. "How new are you?"

"I'm not a sub." *Really fucking new.*

"Oh! I'm sorry, man. I didn't know Master Bradford hired anyone that wasn't a sub to work in the house. I just assumed." Cade laughed. "You like that cross, though. Are you sure you're not subby?"

He wasn't sure of anything at the moment. He eyed the cross....It looked so beautiful and dangerous. "We better get to work, huh?"

Cade nodded. "Sure, yeah. I'll replace the towels. You got the dishwasher?"

"On it." He pulled on gloves and headed into the bathroom. When he returned, hands full of toys, he caught Cade out of the corner of his eye. "Can you open this top drawer for me?"

"Of course."

Wait. Wait, that wasn't Cade's voice. That smooth tone was Bradford's. He looked up sharply.

"Sorry. I hope I didn't startle you. I sent Cade on to the next room."

Bradford opened the drawer and he put away a full set of anal play toys and a clear silicone vibrating cock ring.

"Did you need something?" He pulled off his gloves and set them on top of the cabinet.

"Oh. No, I was just saying good morning to Shiloh in security when I saw you and Cade on the monitor."

He felt himself blush, cheeks growing hot, and he just knew his ears were bright red. "Cade said no one was watching."

"Someone is always watching, Nikki." It seemed like Bradford's voice had just grown deeper.

"I'm sorry if we—"

"No, no. Technically no one broke any rules. That's fine. I just thought, as long as you were here, and you were

obviously so curious, that you might like to try the cross out
—for real."

"For real?"

"With someone you *trust*?"

He looked over his shoulder at the cross, his heart
starting to pound again. "With—"

"Me, Nikki, darling. With me. You trust me, don't you?"
Bradford's voice was so soothing, comforting. It made him
feel safe. He thought he trusted Bradford, at least as much
as he'd ever trusted anyone. More, even.

"I do."

"Do you want to try it out? Just see how it feels? Nothing
more...unless you want more."

He moved slowly toward the cross, his feet going all on
their own.

"That's it, boy. Start by placing your hands flat against it.
As high or low as you wish. That's right. Feel the leather
start to warm under your fingers."

At some point Bradford must have moved to the house
phone by the door, because Nikki heard the conversation
with security.

"You see us on the monitor, Shiloh?...Yes, very good. We
won't need constant visual monitoring, but I wanted to be
sure you were near the intercom in case I need you....Yes,
excellent. Thank you, boy." He heard the click as Bradford
put the phone back in the cradle. "Does the cross feel
warm?"

"Yes." How had he not noticed before the way the
material took on his body heat?

"Lean your body into it. Breathe in that gorgeous
leather."

He did as he was instructed, leaning his torso into the

sturdy center of the cross and stretching his arms up and out.

"That's very nice, boy."

"Thank you."

"Hm." He heard Bradford clear his throat behind him. "Yes. Very good. Tell me, Nikki, do you know what a safe word is?"

"I've heard of them."

"The purpose and intention of safe words are very simple. Your soft word pauses the scene, asks your Dom to step back and slow things down for any reason whatsoever, at any point you are feeling uncomfortable."

"You're...not my Dom." Bradford was not his Dom and he was not a sub. He hadn't consented to that—there had to be consent, right? Bradford had rules.

"No, Nikki, you are correct. However, for the purpose of this demonstration, also known as a scene, I will fill that role. And you, will fill the role of the sub. I will not bind you to this cross without clear safe words from you. Do you understand?"

"Oh." Well, that made sense. "Yes. Okay."

"Good. And then your hard word will stop everything and end the scene entirely. Is that clear?"

"Sure, okay."

"Tell me you understand."

"I understand."

"Good. So, give me your words, boy."

He thought about it. On the one hand, it seemed so silly. Why couldn't he just say "Stop"?

"Um...nickel and dime."

"So be it. Your words are 'nickel' and 'dime.' Thank you, boy."

Bradford was suddenly in motion, and in seconds Nikki's

right hand was bound tightly to the cross, soft padding inside the cuff hugging his wrist.

"Oh!"

"Too tight?"

"Well, no. But…"

"Use your words at any time, boy, if you have concerns." Bradford's fingers made quick work of binding down his other hand as well. "Are you all right?"

He nodded, then wiggled his fingers and looked up the length of one bound arm.

"I require a yes or a no, boy."

"Yes. I'm fine."

Bradford knelt next to him and moments later, his feet were bound as well. "There. You are safe, boy. You are in my hands. I will take care of you."

Nikki pulled gently against his restraints as he listened to Bradford's calm, steady voice.

"I will never leave the room with you bound in any way, I will make sure you know I am here. You are my responsibility, bound as you are, and I take that very seriously."

"Thank you." He wasn't sure why he said it, why he felt he needed to. Bradford's words just moved him to speak. He'd never been taken care of in his life, not even as a child. The idea was comforting now, coming from a man like Bradford—someone who certainly had the means and the confidence to say such things. Someone who had taken time to prove to Nikki that he was honest.

"You are welcome, boy. You look wonderful. The cross suits you. How do you like it?"

"It's—strange."

"Hm." He could hear Bradford's soft footsteps behind

him, just beyond his peripheral vision. "Strange as in new? Or is it that you're not sure yet how you feel?"

"I'm not sure yet...how I feel." He wasn't. His spine was tingling, his heart beating fast.

"You don't know yet what you want."

He shook his head. "I don't. I'm sorry." He was sure Bradford expected more, and he hated to disappoint the man.

Bradford moved around the cross so that Nikki could see his face.

"That's all right, boy," he said softly. "I don't require an apology. You don't have to know, yet. I am just so proud of your willingness to try."

Nikki's breath caught in his throat. Emotion gripped his chest and as he exhaled, he burst into tears.

He felt Bradford step closer. "I'm here, boy. If you want me to release you, use your words."

He shook his head no. He wasn't sure what he did want. He didn't understand the tears, but right now it all felt right. Safe.

Bradford was touching him now; warm hands slid across his skin as Bradford moved around behind him again. "Tears are a release, boy—they are part of this process. I hadn't expected them so soon, but I should be accustomed to that by now. You constantly surprise me."

"I'm sorry...I..." He couldn't get his thoughts out; he was wracked with hitching sobs and his voice wasn't cooperating.

"Shhh. Don't ever apologize for honesty. This is your truth, Nikki. I don't know what it means yet, but we will figure it out together."

He felt both of Bradford's hands settle on his shoulders. "I'm here. You're safe. Just breathe."

Breathe. Just breathe. God, he was so embarrassed.

"That's it. You're fine. I'm right here."

He couldn't remember the last time he'd cried, and he wasn't sure he'd ever sobbed like this before. He felt it in his entire body, and he knew he must look like a complete fool, but there was no stopping the flow of emotion and the physical release. At least Bradford didn't seem to mind. He felt the man's presence everywhere, warm hands on his back, soft words in his ears. Bradford was encouraging him, making him feel safe. Making him feel like this was okay.

He wasn't really okay though, and he suddenly felt completely exhausted, felt his knees give out under him.

"Whoa." Bradford caught him. "Let me get you down from there. I need you to stand, Nikki. Rest your weight against the cross. Just lean in. Good." His feet were suddenly free, and he moved them closer together to better support his own weight. God, he was just so tired. The next thing he knew, he was in Bradford's arms.

"Send me Levi." He heard Bradford say, likely into the intercom. He wrapped his arms around Bradford's neck.

10

Bradford sat by Nikki's bed, watching the boy sleep, feeling anxious. Every so often he'd get up and pace the room, only to find his way back to his chair at the boy's side once more.

With Levi's assistance, they'd brought Nikki to the brownstone, and the boy had allowed Bradford to help him off with his harness and to hold him for a bit before he fell asleep.

For the time being, he just had to hope that he'd done right by the boy. He understood something of what the tears likely meant—he'd seen them under all sorts of circumstances. Tears alone were an interesting thing; there was always so much behind them to explore. Such depth of emotion, such honesty and trust.

Nikki had remained guarded since the day they'd met in the café. He remembered clearly how the boy made the assumption that he would want sex in exchange for a sandwich. He knew he'd intervened just in time, that the boy had been struggling, desperate. He could see it. He knew all too well the pitfalls that had awaited Nikki in this city, as he himself had struggled to avoid every single trap that existed for a teenager on these very streets until his mentor, who would one day become his lover, freed him from that life.

Oh, Harrison. I miss you right now.

He got up to pace again, mulling over everything that had transpired in that room. It was possible that he had intervened too soon, that he ought to have let the boys have their fun and pretended he knew nothing of it. They certainly were not the first subs to explore tools of the trade when left to their own devices. But then again, Nikki wouldn't have let go if the boy hadn't already been overwhelmed. That dam had to have been near breaching without his help. It was better that it happened with him there to catch Nikki, both literally and figuratively.

Nikki had given up a gift the depth of which Bradford had rarely received from any sub. Nikki had literally given up everything. His trust, his truth, his honesty—himself. But it hadn't been an easy gift to give, and the boy was likely to be left raw for it.

Be careful what you wish for, eh, old boy? Now that he had it, he had to be very sure to keep it safe.

Under other circumstances, he would have called his dearest friend and only confidant for advice. Tobias knew him down to his very soul, and the man would have understood his predicament. He wished he could simply pick up the phone and invite Tobias round for a drink or dinner, but the Dom had been absent from the club for months, entirely off the scene as far as he knew. And for reasons that he understood were deeply personal, Tobias had chosen to remain completely out of touch, at least for the time being.

Tobias had thrown himself into his work and his farm, therapy Tobias understandably needed to soothe an aching heart and troubled mind. Bradford didn't feel it would be wise or fair to pull Tobias back into the club so abruptly.

The BDSM scene, however, and the very particular desires of the Dominant man ran deep in Tobias's veins. He'd been a member for just shy of twenty years and, like Bradford, was part of the very soul of the club. Tobias would return eventually, and when he did, Bradford would come up with something—or someone—special for him.

But that was a matter for another day.

He looked at Nikki. The boy's words, the ones he'd been mulling over for an hour, echoed in his mind.

You're not my Dom.

Nikki's words were entirely, and frustratingly, too true. It took every ounce of restraint he'd had in him not to insist that the boy call him "sir" while bound. In light of such a strong objection, however, Nikki's utter lack of reaction to the diminutive term, "boy," was telling. He had been sneaking it into their conversations for the last day or so deliberately, and in his mind, that tacit acceptance had taken the boy much farther down the road to becoming his than Nikki realized.

But these goddamn baby steps were going to be the death of him.

Binding Nikki to that cross was at once thrilling and agonizing. The boy's reaction to the cuffs and the leather and level of unquestioning trust was breathtaking. But his fingers itched to touch Nikki in a more meaningful way, and his arm ached for a whip or a paddle. The boy's emotional catharsis made it very clear, however, even without the whip or any kind of agreement between the two of them, that for Nikki the cross was like accelerating from zero to sixty in seconds. It would be a while before he allowed Nikki to return to that room for a scene.

Still, the boy had been so brave, so willing to step out onto that ledge with him.

Or—was it *for* him?

Oh God, the depth of potential in the beautiful blue-eyed boy was astounding.

He sat again, responsibility weighing heavily on him. The boy could be his. Just a few more tiny steps, a few more fragile moments, and he could have everything he wanted. But Bradford would never allow it to happen at the expense of Nikki's well-being. No, Bradford was going to have to help the boy through this moment, and, he suspected, several more like it before his hopes were realized.

There was a knock at the door and Bradford stood right back up again, making his way out into the hall and closing the door behind him.

"Sorry to interrupt, sir."

"No, that's all right, Levi. What can I do for you?"

"Noah Dolan on the line for you, sir, about Friday. I didn't want to buzz the room and wake up Nikki."

"Good thinking. Yes, I owe him a phone call. Give him my sincere apologies, will you? Tell him that I do have a match to propose to him for Friday, but I'll have to call him later tonight. You can explain that I'm with a sub. He'll understand."

"Oh?" Levi gave him a knowing look. "Are you with a sub, sir?"

Bradford smiled. "Most assuredly, Levi. It's only a matter of time, now."

Great heavens, he sounded like a dirty old man.

How very appropriate.

Levi hurried off to the house phone in the hall and

Bradford headed back into Nikki's room. The bed was empty, and the bathroom light was on.

"Nikki?"

When he didn't get an answer he made his way across the room, realizing about halfway to the door that could hear the shower running. He hesitated a moment, trying to decide if it was better to walk away for now or just poke his head in and ask if the boy needed anything. An anguished sound followed by a heavy sob made his mind up for him.

"Boy?" He burst into the bathroom in full protective mode, brows furrowed and ears tuned to the sobbing coming from behind the shower curtain. He could barely breathe for all the steam and he instantly started to sweat.

"Nikki."

Nikki didn't answer, he just continued to moan and cry while the bathroom filled with steam.

"Goddamnit." He cursed under his breath and reached for the shower curtain, pulling it aside in one smooth motion.

The boy turned to look at Bradford. His hair was wet and hanging in his eyes, his shoulders were hunched and shaking, and he had a miserably defeated look on his face. He turned to face Bradford and leaned in slowly, sobbing against Bradford's chest.

"Oh." He hooked a hand behind Nikki's neck and pulled the boy into his shoulder. Nikki's wet head and the water from the shower quickly soaked through his shirt and splashed onto his trousers, the water so hot it seared his skin.

"Christ, Nikki! What are you doing?" He tried to reach around the boy to shut the water off but he couldn't reach the knobs. "Out. Come on, out. Now, boy."

Nikki obeyed, stepping out of the shower, and it was

only then that he could see how red the boy's skin was. There was no way that hadn't hurt.

He was finally able to reach the taps and shut the water off, and after that he pulled a towel off a rack nearby and wrapped Nikki in it. It was difficult to tell if the boy was still sobbing or shivering while his heated skin mingled with the cooler air.

"Hold on, boy. Let me just..." He took a moment to unbutton and peel off his wet shirt. While he was at it, he kicked off his shoes and dropped his trousers to the floor. He made his way over to the bathroom door and retrieved the thick robe that hung there, wrapping himself in its softness with a sigh. "Okay. I'm going to have a look at your skin, boy." He reached for the towel and removed it, then ran eyes and fingers over Nikki's skin to be sure the boy wasn't injured.

Nikki didn't make a sound or fight him on any of it.

"Well, your skin is very warm to the touch, boy, but it doesn't look like you've damaged yourself." Bradford dried Nikki's hair and toweled off the boy's legs, keeping things as clinical as he could lest he lose himself to the smooth, nearly hairless beauty of the boy's slightly freckled skin, and the impressive heft of Nikki's flaccid cock.

Bradford steered Nikki to the bedroom and got him into a pair of briefs before tucking him back into bed.

He hesitated at the edge of the bed, second-guessing his own instincts.

"Oh, for God's sake." Bradford shook his head at himself. The boy didn't have to be a sub to appreciate his comfort. He climbed up into bed with Nikki and pulled the boy into his arms.

Nikki seemed to rally a bit at that and snuggled into him, resting on his shoulder, one hand on his chest.

"Talk, boy."

"I'm sorry."

"It's quite all right. Tell me what happened—not just now, we'll get to that. Tell me what happened on the cross."

Nikki took a deep breath, and he felt the boy shudder. "I believed you."

Bradford nodded slowly. He thought he knew where Nikki was headed with that, but he wanted the *why*. "You felt safe?"

Nikki nodded against his chest. "My hands and feet were locked to that cross, and I couldn't move, there was no way I could do anything for myself. But you told me I was safe with you, you told me you would take care of me and I just... wanted that so badly. I *want* that so badly."

"For someone else to take responsibility?"

"Yes."

"For someone to take care of you." *See to your needs, help you learn yourself. A Dom.*

"Yes. For the doubt to go away. For the worry to stop."

"Worry."

"About being alone. About never finding—"

"Family." He didn't mean to put words in the boy's mouth, but he knew. He knew exactly what Nikki was telling him.

"Yes."

"For someone to tell you that you belong."

Oh, God.

Nikki didn't just remind him of the young man he once was, the shelter kid his mentor rescued many years ago. Nikki essentially *was* that young man.

"Yes." Nikki sat up and looked at Bradford, wonder in his sapphire eyes.

"Someone you trust."

"I trust you."

"Thank you, boy." Inside he was cheering. "So, in that moment you believed me, that I would look after you, that I would keep you safe."

"I realized that I had no choice, so I just...and it was so...I felt so light. I was bound to that cross, but I felt so free." Nikki sighed and settled that blond head against his chest again. "You made me feel free."

He'd been quite right, and also somewhat wrong about this boy. All his careful consideration and he still hadn't come close to figuring Nikki out. The cross wasn't too much for the boy. It wasn't too much at all. If anything, it was a springboard to deeper discovery. Nikki had a capacity for submission that he was only beginning to grasp, and Bradford couldn't wait to dive in further.

"And the shower?"

Nikki shook his head. "I don't know. I wanted a shower. But once I got in I just kept turning the cold tap down until I'd turned it off completely. I don't know, I wasn't thinking really, I just...did it."

He knew. He absolutely knew that it was time to get this boy into a scene. A real one. Into a scene and out of his own head.

He hugged Nikki to him and stroked fingers through the boy's damp hair.

"I want to talk with you about something Nikki, but not now. Not while you're emotional. Perhaps in a couple of days when you're feeling better, you would have dinner with me again?"

"Oh, sure. Dinner was really good."

Bradford smiled. "Good."

Nikki sighed. "I'm starving."

Bradford laughed. Oh, to be twenty again when, despite everything, your stomach was still your highest priority. "Let's get you a burger then, boy."

11

B radford did love to throw a party, and like every good Leo, he loved his birthday too. The middle of July meant it was time to start planning for his Big Birthday Bash. He threw himself a lavish party every year, always with a different theme, and frequently with outside entertainment. He'd decided that this year's party was going to be a grand black-and-white masked ball: Doms in black, subs in white.

The summer was typically the quietest season for the club, and the hot months dragged on without many occasions for celebration. Toward the end of August, members started to reappear from whatever summer retreats they'd escaped to and were looking to reconnect and reengage. It was the perfect time for a soiree.

But just a day after Nikki's first real submissive breakthrough, he wasn't able to concentrate on celebrations. He closed the folder on his desk and tapped his fingers on it, trying with little success to clear his mind.

His desk phone rang, an outside line, and he knew Levi would pick it up. Moments later, however, his phone buzzed.

"For me?"

"Yes, sir. Noah Dolan, sir."

"Oh, for the love of...I forgot to call him back. Thank you, Levi, I'll take it."

"Yes, sir. Line four."

Bradford sighed and shook his head. Noah had been frustrated with his experience at the club of late and was close enough to giving up his membership already. Losing a sub of Noah's caliber could be damaging from a business perspective and simply bad form from a personal one.

"Good afternoon, Noah," Bradford said smoothly.

"Master Bradford. You're a hard man to reach."

"Entirely my fault, Noah. I've been occupied with a sub who is in a very delicate place and it's had me distracted."

"I hope he is all right?"

"He's doing better, thank you. Kind of you to think of him. I think things are improving."

"Good to hear."

"But that isn't why you called. I apologize for my excuses. You are calling about Friday?"

"Yeah. Levi told me you might have a match in mind?"

"I do. He's a charter member of the club, highly experienced."

"Sounds promising."

Noah was employed in law enforcement and, from what Bradford understood, had a regular downtown beat. Calling during his workday meant that he was on duty. Bradford had learned not to expect the deference Noah would, of course, give to a Dom at other times. At one of his early membership interviews, Noah drew a hard line when it came to his personal time. It was important to the boy that he not be required to respond as a sub should 24/7. Their agreement was that Noah was a cop outside of the confines of the club, and Bradford respected that. He certainly wasn't the only one.

"Before I get in too far with my suggestions, Noah, let me clarify with you once more my understanding of what you're looking for?"

"Sure, go ahead."

"You're still looking to find a long-term Dom, someone looking for a contract?"

"Ideally. I'm not getting what I need from these one-off evenings, you know?"

"Yes, I understand." That request in itself was a tall order. It cut out half his Dominant members right off the bat, and despite his knack for bringing men together, Bradford didn't much care for playing matchmaker for long-term arrangements, either. But he'd had this sort of request before, and he had some idea how to go about helping Noah find what he needed.

"Even if I could just find someone regular, you know? A standing Friday night session, some way to get to know the D...the *guy* better, work on a rapport. Dig deeper."

Noah was nothing if not deep. During Noah's early days at the club, Bradford worked with him exclusively for a couple of weeks, as he did with every new sub that professed to be experienced. Noah's presentation was perfect; there was nothing he could teach the boy in that regard, and he knew immediately that there wasn't a Dom in the stable that wouldn't be satisfied by a session. But Noah never relaxed with him, not completely, nor had the boy been able to do so with any other Dom he'd paired with Noah since.

"Yes, I understand, Noah."

"They can't be satisfied just with what feels good."

He nodded. That was it, wasn't it? Noah needed

someone to push him past good enough, past common expectations. "They need to challenge you."

"Yes."

"How?"

"I'm sorry?"

"How do you want to be pushed? Is there a particular boundary you want to work on?"

"I..." Noah sighed. "Yeah, um. That's the thing, I don't know. I'm not sure where my limits are right now. I need help to figure that out."

"Hm."

"I'm sorry, Master Bradford. But that is exactly the issue, I think."

"Not to worry, boy. I hear what you're telling me." One thing he could count on from Noah, at least, was honesty. Sometimes to a fault.

"What do you know about Master Reed?"

"Um, he's older, been there a while, has a reputation for hitting hard."

"All right. Yes, as I said, he is a charter member. He's been with the club longer than I have. Longer than almost anyone." He'd been a good friend of Harrison's, back in the day. "His strengths lie in the heavy-hitting tools. He's very demanding, he won't allow you to get away with anything—he won't settle—and he doesn't let up until he's had enough, or he thinks he's pushed you nearly to your words. His scenes are dynamic and intense."

"Wow."

"Mm. He's not for the faint of heart, my boy, I promise you that. And he'll use every verbal tool in the handbook to keep you off balance—demands, humiliation, praise, coercion, anger, encouragement, abuse, you name it. You'll have to work for sure. But whether that will help you accomplish your goals, whether you'll find a boundary, I couldn't say. You won't get off easy, though, and I believe he'll at least get you out of your head."

"He knows what I need?"

"He will. And I know he will attempt to push you. I'll be sure he sees your file and understands your few hard limits."

"Well. He sounds intimidating."

To say the least. "What good is a Dom that isn't, my boy?"

Noah laughed. "Okay, terrifying."

"Mhm. That's a fair assessment. So, what do you think?"

"I'm interested."

"Excellent. Let's give this a try and see if Reed can at least help you clarify things for yourself."

"Great. Thanks, Master Bradford."

Now for the important bit. "One tip, Noah. If you want to impress him at the outset, dress."

"Like a tie?"

"Like a tie and a jacket. And a clean shave. He'll take you more seriously."

"Thanks for the tip."

"Good day."

"Bye, sir."

Bradford put down the phone. He'd thought long and hard about this match. He remembered his own training with Reed—the only way to describe him was relentless. Reed was older now, well into his sixties, but just as in shape as ever. He knew Noah could handle the intensity, and he knew Reed would be pleased with the boy. He just didn't know if the pair could find what it was Noah was looking for.

12

T he dining room was buzzing. It was Friday night and the club was fairly busy for a summer weekend, but that wasn't what had everyone excited. Bradford knew damn well that it was his own fault the boys were all wound up. He had a dinner reservation, which was common enough for a Friday night, but what wasn't common was that he had dressed for the occasion.

He was wearing leather.

He had several bespoke and made-to-measure suits and indulged himself in frequent visits from his tailor. He rarely went in for the signature uniforms of his trade, preferring silk to leather, especially in the summer months. Typically that worked in his favor, setting him apart from the other Doms at the club on a busy night, enforcing his position as Host and MC, and commanding at a glance the respect the owner of a gentleman's club deserved.

But tonight, he had negotiations on his mind with a boy he'd had his eye on for months and he wanted everyone, including Nikki, to take him for every inch of the Dominant that he was. Still, he wasn't terribly far from his comfort zone, having chosen a custom-tailored leather sport jacket to wear over a simple, fitted, black cotton T-shirt and leather pants. He wasn't a fan of heavy boots either and instead wore a pair of shiny, black leather dress shoes.

He certainly understood the psychology behind heavy-heeled boots, leather vests, and ink. But he liked to play a different game, and it had always served him well. Tonight, it was serving him very well indeed, and he hadn't even seen Nikki yet.

"Bradford."

"Reed!" He reached out and shook the man's hand. "Are you finished with your dinner already?"

"I am. The boy and I had a good talk, and we are both anxious to begin."

Now that Reed had mentioned the boy, he allowed himself to look at Noah, who was standing just beyond Reed's left shoulder. He had to smile; the boy had dressed as they'd discussed, though at this point Reed held Noah's tie and suit jacket in one hand and the boy's shirt was unbuttoned to midtorso. In Reed's other hand was a leash attached to a set of tame but heavy nipple clamps on Noah's chest.

"One moment." He looked around quickly and found Jamison helping Joe restock at the bar. "Jamison, come here, boy."

"Yes, sir!" The boy put the bottle that was in his hands down on the bar and headed straight over, going to his knees at Bradford's feet.

Leather. Bradford shook his head.

"On your feet, boy."

"Yes, sir."

"Reed." Bradford reached for Noah's jacket and tie and Reed handed them over. "Jamison, run these up to the heavy bondage room on the third floor. Hurry now. Leave them neatly on the red chair and run back. Stay out of Master Reed's way."

"Yes, sir." Jamison took the clothing and literally ran.

"Thank you, Bradford. That simplifies things a bit."

"And you'll look much better ascending the stairs," he said knowingly.

Reed's laughter was genuine. "Oh, you are clever, my friend."

Bradford winked at him. "Just doing my job."

"Are you? You seem dressed for more."

"Ah. Yes, I have plans myself this evening."

"Excellent."

Jamison returned quickly but slowed to a walk as he passed Bradford and Reed, eyes low and back straight.

"Thank you, boy."

"My pleasure, sir. Enjoy your evening, Master Reed."

"Don't let me hold you up any longer, Reed. I know you've both got goals this evening. Best get to it."

"Indeed." Reed nodded to him and began to walk without warning, giving the leash a deliberate tug.

Noah hissed.

"Sloppy already, boy, and the night is so young."

"I'm sorry, sir."

He grinned as they headed for the stairwell. Noah had followed perfectly to heel; Reed could be a bastard when he wanted to be. Bradford watched them walk up the stairs, admiring Noah's technique—eyes low, chin level, expression still, back straight. The Doms in this club were lining up to work with the boy, and yet Noah couldn't find one that suited his needs. Ordinarily, Bradford would assume that meant the sub was too hard to please, but he'd worked with Noah. The boy wasn't dismissing these Doms lightly. Noah just had a specific need that wasn't being met. A hunger. He'd be dedicated—devoted, even—to the right man.

"Master Bradford, your table is ready, sir."

"Hm?" He looked around and found Brian kneeling at his feet. What was it about the leather?

"Up, boy."

"Your table is ready, sir."

"Very good, Brian. Thank you." Bradford could feel the boy practically vibrating beside him as they walked.

"Are you meeting anyone this evening, Brian?"

"Yes, sir."

"Well, thank goodness for that. You need it."

"Yes, sir. Thank you, sir."

"Hm." Bradford snorted. Brian pulled out his chair. "Bring me an ice water. You will send Nikki directly here when you see him."

"Yes, sir." Brian disappeared.

He unbuttoned his jacket and hung it over the back of his chair. It was warm enough in here without being wrapped in cowhide. He took a seat and looked around the room, nodding now and then to any Dom that caught his eye. He was at his usual table in the middle of the room and if he were a betting man, he would guess that he was the new topic of conversation at most of the others—well he, and the subject of his mystery guest.

They didn't have to wait long. When Bradford looked up again, Brian was on his way with his water and with Nikki as well.

He stood, trying not to let himself look as winded as he suddenly felt. He'd sent Nikki a pair of leather pants as a gift with no demand that the boy wear them, but Nikki had. They fit like a glove and paired nicely with the tight white T-shirt and low black boots the boy had chosen. He was well aware of the eyes on them both as he shook hands with Nikki and invited the boy to sit down.

"Thank you for coming."

"I told you I would."

"Indeed." But he hadn't counted on anything, hadn't dared.

"The pants are totally cool. I love them."

He smiled. "I was hoping you might. They seem to fit you well." It was just as well that he hadn't gotten a look at Nikki's ass in them yet; the front had his blood pressure up as it was.

Nikki picked up his menu and looked it over.

"You may wish to eat light," he suggested. "Depending on how our conversation goes, you might not want a full stomach later."

Nikki looked at him over the menu, then closed it and lowered it slowly to the table again. "Oh?"

There was little point in delaying this—the rest of his evening, and Nikki's, depended on the outcome of their discussion. He leaned forward, crossing his arms on the table and looking into Nikki's deep sapphire eyes. He was careful to keep his voice low.

"I want to contract with you, Nikki."

Nikki blinked at him. "Contract with me?"

"For one evening. One night. Tonight."

"I'm not sure what you're asking me."

He nodded. "I'd like to negotiate an evening of play with you. Upstairs. I am asking you to sub for me tonight."

He watched the boy carefully, observing how Nikki's breath quickened, and the skin at the boy's throat began to flush.

"Sub for you."

"Yes. We would negotiate mutually agreeable terms of

course; you can set whatever limits you need." He knew perfectly well the boy wouldn't know what limits to set, but he had a very simple evening in mind, nothing that should rattle Nikki or frustrate him too greatly.

The blush made its way into the boy's cheeks and Nikki swallowed. "So...a scene? Like the other day?"

"Just so, yes. Only you'd be my sub. We would be working together in a real scene. I would have a responsibility to you, and you to me."

Nikki looked down at his hands, thoughtfully. "I think I'd like that."

He forcefully swallowed down the elation he felt at hearing those words. Now was not the time.

Steady, man. Steady. He's almost yours.

He did allow himself to smile, however. "Wonderful. I reserved the St. Andrews room again if—"

"Yes. Can we...I mean, I'd like to..."

"Explore that further?"

"Explore that further," Nikki agreed, using his words. But the boy wasn't mocking him this time. "Yes."

"Excellent. Let's set some boundaries, shall we? I can start, that might help you." Bradford leaned back in his chair again and sipped his ice water. "For tonight, I will not use any tools intended to cause any manner of discomfort. I would like to work with sensory tools, they'll make your skin tingle or tickle and become very sensitive, but without pain. For this I require you naked, as I'll need access to your skin. And I think we should keep this first encounter short, hm?"

Nikki nodded.

"Tell me what you want."

"I want to be tied...uh, *restrained*."

He allowed himself another grin. What fun listening to the boy practice the vocabulary. "Yes, and?"

"I think the sensitive or uh…"

"Sensory?"

"Yeah. Sensory work sounds interesting. I'm not sure how I feel about much more than that yet."

"Understood."

"And no sex."

He leaned forward and put his glass down on the table before he dropped it. "No sex. By which you mean no fucking? No fellatio? No touching? Where's your line, boy?"

"No sex at all."

"At all." He raised an eyebrow but otherwise tried to hide his dismay at that request. He'd intended to demand a blowjob of the boy at least….Ah. How foolish of him to assume. Well, if that was the boy's hard line, so be it. Tonight was not the night for a true negotiation; he didn't want to scare the boy off with too many demands. "Very well."

"Do you promise?"

"Do I—" He snorted, incensed, and unable to stop himself this time. "Boy, we've just made a gentleman's agreement; there's no need for promises."

"Promise me."

He eyed the boy, reminding himself yet again that this was Nikki's first negotiation, and the boy obviously had some kind of hang-up about sex Bradford was unaware of. He would have to explore the issue another time. "All right, boy. I promise."

Nikki nodded. "Okay, then."

He raised two fingers in the air. Brian was at his side in an instant. "The small plate for the boy and I will have the sautéed scallops, please."

"Yes, sir." Brian hurried off.

"You're ordering for me?"

"I am. Brian will bring you a plate of light but nourishing bites to give you energy without weighing you down. You'll thank me, I promise."

"Okay..." Nikki looked skeptical.

"One more very important thing, boy."

"What is it?"

"Once we begin, you must only call me 'sir' or 'Master.' Further, after this first contract, that level of respect must continue indefinitely, as with all the other subs at the club, whether we are currently bound by an agreement or not. Do you understand?"

"All the time?"

"Always."

Nikki looked thoughtful but didn't take long to agree. "Okay. I can do that."

"They are not just words, Nikki. Any Dom in the club will have the right to come to me if you are disrespectful to them. And I will have the prerogative to punish you."

"Punish me?"

"Not to worry, boy. I will honor your learning curve. 'Punishment' for the time being will be a mere discussion. That will change, of course, as you grow into your service."

"*If* I do."

He nodded once. "If you do. And I hope you do."

And you will. I know you will.

"What is punishment for Brian?"

"He rarely needs it, but generally it would start at two lashes with a crop of my choosing and increase from there depending on the severity of the offense."

"Ow."

He shrugged. "That's really nothing for Brian. Every sub

is different. I wouldn't hit Levi, for example. I would humiliate him."

"Why?"

"Levi draws a hard limit at being hit. Pain doesn't fall within his scope of interest or meet his needs. He takes great pride in his service, and so an apt punishment for him would be to make it clear that his service didn't meet my expectations. A step further would be to do so publicly." Good lord, that would probably reduce the poor boy to tears.

"Wow."

"Though honestly, I can't begin to imagine punishing Levi. There's not a Dom at this club that ever has in earnest, as far as I know. I certainly haven't."

"So if I wanted to, you know, continue...I could really set whatever limits I want?"

"Of course, boy. Your body, your mind, your limits."

Nikki seemed to take that in, looking thoughtful. "Okay. So what now?"

He smiled. "Now, we eat."

Brian set out their plates, refilled their water glasses, and moved away swiftly. The boy had been around long enough to know what negotiations looked like and knew better than to linger. Bradford gave Nikki some time to relax while he ate, enjoying the electricity that was building between them in the silence.

When Nikki looked about done, he put down his fork. "This is what will happen next. Listen carefully, I'm only going to tell you once. I don't expect you to be perfect in any way, boy, but I do expect you to try your hardest. I want everyone in this room to believe in your sincerity, to see how much you want to please me."

Nikki looked up at him, placed his fork on his plate, and his hands in his lap. "Okay."

"The appropriate response is, 'Yes, sir.' "

Nikki sighed heavily. "Yes, sir."

"Good. Now lower your eyes. You don't have to look at the ground, but you are not to meet anyone's eyes, is that understood? For tonight that will include other subs. No eye contact. Repeat that for me and end with, 'sir.' "

"Eyes low, no eye contact with anyone. Yes, sir."

Bradford smiled. "That was perfect, my boy. Very nice."

"Thank you, sir."

Oh, they were off to a good start.

"When I stand, you will stand. Do your best to walk behind my right shoulder. <u>Behind</u> me—not on my heels; we'll have to work on that skill, and I don't want either of us to be tripped up tonight with all these eyes on you."

"On *me*?"

He gave the boy an expectant look, one eyebrow lifting in question.

"On me, *sir*?" Nikki corrected.

"Yes, boy. You are headed upstairs for a scene with the owner of this club. Trust me, I'm not being arrogant when I say that people are curious. They will be watching." Well, maybe he was being somewhat arrogant, but it was true nonetheless.

"Okay...uh. I understand, sir."

"Very nice."

Nikki took a deep breath. He looked absolutely terrified.

"You're going to do fine, boy. I will never ask of you anything I don't believe you are capable of handling."

Nikki nodded. "Okay. Thank you, sir."

"Now, when you are ready—and not a moment sooner —you will stand up, straighten yourself up, and then silently come kneel next to my chair. Remember, eyes low. A few moments later I will stand, and we will go. I won't say anything. I'll just expect you to follow. Clear?"

"Kneel, then follow you. Yes, sir."

"Eyes low."

"Eyes low. Yes, sir."

"This is a gift you're giving me, Nikki, and I will treat it with care. You have my word. Now, whenever you're ready, boy. Take your time."

Nikki took one last sip of his water and a deep breath. When the boy stood, he heard the room go quiet and felt the eyes in the room turn to them both. He kept his gaze glued to his sub, following Nikki's every move.

Nikki straightened his T-shirt and smoothed out his leather, then stepped over next to Bradford's chair and dropped to his knees. The silence was broken by a few small gasps, and the room filled with conversation again.

He sipped his water as well. Eventually, he stood up, slowly pulled on his jacket, and headed out of the room. He resisted the urge to look back and make sure Nikki was following. It was the boy's first test, and it was not nearly as easy as it sounded. He nodded to several Doms as he passed their tables, shook one or two hands when they were offered, and made his way out of the dining room.

As they climbed the stairs to the second floor, Bradford turned and looked in the mirror at the boy. Nikki's eyes were low, and he was only a step behind, but his back was stiff as a board and his hands were trembling. Bradford picked up the pace, moving down the long hall to the St. Andrews room as quickly as possible and keyed open the door.

"Come, boy." He herded the boy inside and closed the door. "All right. Breathe, boy. Breathe. That's done, and you did just fine. Look where you like, sit, stand, walk, whatever you need. Go ahead and let it out. It was a lot, I understand."

The social pressure that came along with subbing for him could be daunting, but he was concerned at Nikki's level of anxiety. It seemed excessive, even for a new sub.

Nikki pressed the heels of his hands over his eyes. "I was just really nervous. Really, really, nervous. I don't like being..."

"The center of attention."

"Not at all." Nikki moved his hands and blinked and shook his fingers out in front of him.

Bradford forgave the lack of respectful terms for the moment, focusing instead on the horrible stage fright his boy seemed to be struggling with. The show tonight was necessary and unavoidable, both as a first test for Nikki and to cement the boy's status at the club, but he made a mental note to hold off on further parades of that sort for a while. "Well, you did it, boy. It was a long walk, but it's over. You did very well. I am proud of you." He reached out and rubbed a hand across Nikki's shoulders. Nikki turned to him instantly, seeking comfort, and in moments Bradford had both of his arms around the boy. "You're safe, boy. Listen to me. You're alone with me now, I will take care of you."

"Yes, sir."

"Believe it, boy."

"I do, sir."

"Good boy." He let Nikki go. "Let's get started then. It will do both of us good. Strip for me, fold your clothes, and place them on top of that chest. Put your boots by the door. I'm going to check in with security."

"Yes, sir." He paused a moment, watching Nikki move, noting the stiffness in the boy's shoulders had diminished some. He also noted a little smugly that Nikki had fallen easily into using 'sir' again as soon as the boy felt safe. He crossed to the house phone and called security.

"Good evening, sir. You're settled in?"

"Yes, Pat, thank you. We'll be working, but I expect it to be an early evening." Especially since he wouldn't be fucking anyone.

Dammit.

"Very good, sir. We've got eyes. Enjoy your evening."

Bradford hung up the phone and turned around to find that Nikki had walked over to the cross and was standing in front of it. Bradford smiled.

Oh-ho. And so it begins.

"No, pup. Over here, please." He pointed to the cuffs that hung at the other end of the room.

"Oh, but—"

" 'Yes sir,' will do. Thank you."

"Yes, sir." Nikki's disappointment was adorable. Truly.

"What are your words, boy?"

"Nickel and dime, sir."

Bradford lowered the cuffs to Nikki's shoulder height and secured a wrist into each one. The cuffs he'd requested be set up for him were very wide, six inches or so, and lined with a thick layer of synthetic fur. They covered most of Nikki's forearms.

" 'Nickel and dime.' It is my responsibility to keep you safe, boy, but you have to help me do that. If your fingers begin to fall asleep or the cuffs begin to bind and are uncomfortable, you are to tell me immediately. You may respectfully interrupt me at any point or use your soft word if you can't manage that. Am I clear?"

"Yes, sir."

"If your arms become fatigued or begin to ache, you should let me know as well."

"Yes, sir."

"Stand arm's length from the wall, hands flat against it, shoulder height, feet wide apart." Bradford moved to the chest. He took off his jacket, hung it up, and kicked off his shoes and socks. He pulled open a drawer, removing a three-row pinwheel, a leather blindfold, a small padded leather paddle, and a short-handled feather teaser. He stuck everything into various pockets except for the blindfold.

"Good boy. I'm going to cover your eyes," he said, moving in behind Nikki. "It will be easier on you than keeping them closed for our session, and by denying one of your senses, the others become more acute." He placed the blindfold over Nikki's eyes and tied it on; then he reached around and spread the leather out for maximum coverage. "Can you see, boy? I don't want any light peeking in."

"No, sir."

"Remember to use your words if you need them. I'm right here. If you can't feel me, you will be able to hear me. You will not be alone. You are safe."

"Thank you, sir."

Nikki didn't seem nervous about the lack of vision, so Bradford jumped right in, running the feather teaser over the boy's shoulders. "All you need to do, boy, is listen, feel, and breathe. That's all I will require of you tonight." He was using his most soothing voice, low and smooth, speaking slowly, musically. "Listen. Feel. Breathe." He kept up his work with the tickler, first one shoulder, then the other. "Repeat that, boy."

"Listen, feel, and breathe, sir."

"I'm not hearing you breathe." He grinned. Sometimes the most difficult part was the breathing.

Nikki took in a deep breath and let it out slowly.

"That's it, boy. How does this feel?"

"Soft, sir. Tickles a little."

"Feel," Bradford said softly. "Listen."

Nikki nodded.

"Submission can be a very complicated thing, Nikki. But it can also be this simple. I asked you what you wanted, you told me you wanted to be restrained. But I'm your Dom, so the how and the where are up to me. How long is up to me. What happens next is up to me, mostly—we agreed on no pain and no intimate play this evening, but within our stated limits the rest is up to my imagination. You have given up control to me, to use you as I please."

This was good for him too. It had been a long time since he'd broken it down and gone back to basics, pulling out the sensual tools and paying attention to the simple details. Bradford worked the teaser over Nikki's shoulders again and again in relentless circles, smiling as the boy's skin began to visibly warm. "Breathe."

Nikki took in a deep breath and let it out slowly. His shoulders were relaxed now, his weight braced against the wall. Bradford lifted the teaser away and blew air gently across Nikki's skin, earning a sigh.

"Good boy." He went right back to running the teaser across Nikki's shoulders again, drawing circles, figure eights, spinning the tool in his fingers and keeping constant contact with Nikki's skin.

"Feel."

"Feels good, sir."

"The same?"

"No. No, it's different, now. It's more...intense, and I can even feel some of the individual feathers now."

"Your skin is becoming more sensitive."

"Just feels good, sir."

"Good boy." He didn't let up. When Nikki's skin was

starting to blush hard in the couple of places he had gone over the most, he put away the teaser and pulled out the pinwheel.

Gingerly, so as not to startle the boy, He set the pinwheel down on the far right side of one shoulder, and applying minimal pressure, he began to roll it across toward the other side.

Nikki shivered and his skin broke out in goose bumps. Bradford eased up a little, but he didn't stop. "Breathe."

Nikki took a deep breath, and Bradford pointed the pinwheel toward a particularly pink patch of skin.

"Oh." Nikki gasped. That was lovely enough, but the boy's gasp was followed by a soft moan, and he felt pride swell in his chest.

"Beautiful, my boy."

"Sir, what is that?"

"Do you like it?"

"Yes, sir. Makes me tingle."

"It's called a Wartenberg wheel, or a pinwheel. I'll show it to you later." He increased the pressure and rolled the wheel over the same spot on the other shoulder. He continued, slowly but firmly rolling the pinwheel over Nikki's sensitive skin, which only grew more sensitive by the moment. He stopped speaking, letting Nikki's breathing be organic, letting the boy begin to float. Nikki's responses grew along with his sensitivity until his moans became more intense and nearly continuous.

At that point he stopped and put the pinwheel aside, turning back to the teaser. He drew the feathers over one of Nikki's shoulders, and the boy shivered and moaned loudly, shrinking away slightly from the touch.

So goddamn beautiful.

He did it again on the other shoulder and this time Nikki whimpered.

"Sir!"

"Too much, boy?" He tossed the teaser aside with the pinwheel. Nikki had done good work, and Bradford didn't want to push the boy beyond the limits of their agreement.

"It...stings, sir. Like needles. Hurts."

"Do you like it?"

"Sir."

"I've put it away, boy. It's only a question."

"I...I think? It was just so intense."

"Well, we drew a line at pain tonight, boy. But perhaps we can explore that sensation another time."

Nikki nodded. The zing of the feathers on sensitive skin jarred him enough to speak but now that moment was past, the boy was back to that lovely space he'd been in before his evil little experiment.

Bradford admired his work: the very pink skin around the boy's shoulders that would stay tender through the night, standing out in contrast to the paleness of the skin on the rest of his torso and lower back.

Concerned the boy was too floaty to know whether his fingers were asleep, Bradford gently removed the cuffs one at a time, leaving Nikki's hands braced on the wall.

At first he thought Nikki hadn't noticed, but then the boy rallied. "Sir..."

"Still with me, boy?"

"Yes, sir."

Bradford questioned that and removed the blindfold. Nikki's skin was covered in a lovely light sweat, particularly around his brow and hairline, and Bradford dropped the damp blindfold on the floor with the other tools he'd used.

"Tell me how you feel."

"I'm fine, sir."

"That's not what I asked, boy. Tell me exactly how you feel. I want details."

"I, um. I feel...light, like my feet aren't quite on the floor. My shoulders are hot, tender, super sensitive. I can feel your breath on them."

He wasn't standing that close. The boy really was sensitive.

"How are your hands?"

"My..."

"Move your arms, boy. Wiggle your fingers."

"Yes, sir." Nikki did as requested. "They are fine, sir."

"Good boy. Do you feel safe?"

"Yes, sir."

"Do you trust me?"

"Yes, sir."

"Do you wish to please me, boy?"

"Yes, sir. I do."

"Good boy. Come." Bradford took Nikki by the hand and led him across the room to the cross. "I have a reward in mind for you, for your good work with the pinwheel and for your earnest submission to my will this evening."

"Thank you, sir."

"Step up to the cross, arms up. Your shoulders may ache a little as you raise them. Breathe and use your words if you need them."

Nikki followed Bradford's order, settling against the cross easily, and raising his arms up the length of the cross. If the raw skin on his shoulders was bothering the boy at all, he didn't complain.

"Very nice." He quickly bound Nikki's hands in place. "You will tell me if any of the bonds are too tight."

"Yes, sir."

He locked the ankle cuffs as well. "The cross is your reward, boy. There is no doubt in my mind that there is a reason you are drawn to it, and I intend to help you begin to learn why."

"Thank you, sir."

He took a deep breath as he walked a slow circle around the cross. "Give me your words again."

"Nickel and dime, sir."

"You will use them if you need them."

"Yes, sir."

He stopped and held up the paddle where Nikki could see it. "This paddle is soft and thuddy, it won't hurt the first few times, but the effect will be cumulative. I'm going to use it on your ass, boy, until I've had enough or until you use your words. Understand?"

Nikki's eyes were on the paddle. "Yes, sir."

"Relax, boy. Trust me. You're in the right space for this."

"I trust you, sir."

He felt his own shoulders relaxing with the first couple of taps to Nikki's ass. He'd spent so much time reassuring and focusing on Nikki, he didn't realize he'd grown so tense. Bradford paced behind Nikki and then added two more, the thump of the soft paddle satisfying his senses.

"Okay, boy?"

"Yes, sir. Fine, sir."

He nodded. He'd fix that.

He started in with the paddle again, varying the location and intensity of the strokes but keeping his rhythm constant. Thump after thump, he laid into Nikki's ass until it was pink and hot and the little gasps and grunts he'd been getting from Nikki turned to sighs and groans.

There wasn't a muscle in Nikki's body that wasn't relaxed

or anything about the boy's posture that would lead Bradford to believe he was anywhere near his safe word.

Time for the rest of the boy's reward.

"You have done beautifully tonight, boy." He let up on the intensity of the strokes, but not the frequency. "I asked you to trust and you have. I asked you to believe that I would keep you safe, and you did. You have let me bind you, use you, even hit you, and all because it pleases me. You didn't question or express reservation." He slowed his arm, the taps barely touching the boy. "You have earned your time on the cross, and you have satisfied my every request."

"Thank you, sir."

He stepped away, putting the paddle and the other instruments he'd used aside to be cleaned, essentially just wasting time and letting Nikki breathe while the boy returned to the room. Nikki had done very well, but it was time to see just how successful their evening had been.

"Nikki?"

"Yes, sir." Nikki's voice was soft, his tone compliant.

"I'm going to undo your cuffs now."

"Thank you, sir."

He took his time, removing each of Nikki's restraints and admiring his work. Nikki's shoulders were still warm and pink, and now his ass had a lovely blush to match. Just gorgeous. So pretty he almost didn't miss the blowjob he'd originally planned.

Almost.

Dammit.

Nikki lowered his hands to his side but otherwise waited for Bradford's instructions.

"Kneel, boy."

He held out a hand to assist the boy on the way down

and Nikki placed a hand in his palm as invited, but really didn't need the help. "Thank you, sir."

"You're welcome, boy."

When Nikki didn't let go of his hand, he bent and gently put the boy's hand down himself. He got a little whimper, but Nikki didn't move.

"Tell me who you are."

"Nikki, sir."

"Yes, boy. Usually. Who are you right now?"

"I'm yours, sir."

His chest went tight and he had to physically pace away from Nikki. *He doesn't understand what he is saying.* He reminded himself. *Not yet.*

He wanted those words to be their truth. Eventually. But right now...

He took a deep breath and let it out slowly, willing himself back to center. It was a shame that the rest of his body was not as adept at following his orders as his subs tended to be.

"You are my sub, boy."

"Yes, sir. I am your sub."

"And I?"

"You are my Dom, sir."

"I am. How do those truths make you feel? Take your time."

Nikki was quiet for a moment, but it didn't take him long to express himself clearly. "Safe. Cared for. Wanted."

He nodded, not surprised by the boy's choice of words. "Well done, boy. There's a lovely oatmeal-scented lotion in the first aid cabinet. Retrieve that and two bottles of water, please, and then come sit with me."

The lotion was completely unnecessary from a first aid perspective, but he liked it for aftercare. The scent was soothing, and Nikki would appreciate the touches. He turned and moved to a divan in the far corner and took a seat in the center, patting his knees as Nikki did as he'd asked and made his way over as well.

"Across my knees, boy."

Nikki stretched out over his lap, pillowing his head on his arms at one end of the divan. He pretended not to notice that the boy was half-hard, but he certainly did. It was interesting that Nikki was so intimidated by the prospect of physical intimacy and yet didn't seem to be the least bit body-shy. Perhaps that promise really was enough for him. If so, that level of trust would take the pair of them very far.

He squeezed some lotion into his palm and spread it across both hands, warming it as it distributed through his fingers. By the time he laid his slippery hands on Nikki's back, the lotion was very warm.

"Mm." Nikki hummed happily as Bradford worked the lotion into his shoulders.

"This time after a scene, after we've gone wherever we need to for the evening, this is our time to relax and recover. You'll feel yourself returning from what we call subspace, and what's important is that you should feel free to talk about anything that comes to mind. It might be related to our scene, or it might not. Or you might find you don't wish to speak at all and that's fine, too. I've known subs to take hours, overnight, a day or even more to feel completely restored. Just take your time and know I'm here. There is no wrong way."

He was reminded of a scene that he and Tobias's former boy, Phantom, had indulged in together a couple of months ago. He'd had to clear his calendar for a full day to recover with Phan and then took a second day to continue taking care of the boy. They'd both needed something that night, and though he didn't often care to go as far as Phan was capable, when he had that particular itch to scratch, he knew precisely who to call.

He continued working lotion into Nikki's skin, moving down the sub's back and over that lovely pink ass. The boy blushed beautifully. All that pale skin was just begging for some color. He took his time; he never watched a clock when he worked a scene, and Nikki was welcome to as much of his time as needed.

Though Bradford couldn't be sure what to infer from the boy's silence.

He was just finishing off his water when Nikki stretched out, long and lean, in his lap. "Oh, that felt so good, sir."

"The lotion?"

"Yes, sir."

"And everything else?"

"Amazing. Just incredible. Thank you, sir."

He nodded approvingly. "You may sit up if you wish, boy."

Nikki did just that, standing in fact and stretching tall before taking a seat beside him again. He handed the boy a bottle of water, and Nikki drank half of it down in one gulp.

"You heard everything I said about talking if you like?"

"Yes, sir. But I have so much swirling around in my head, I can't pin any of it down yet."

"That's quite all right. Let's plan to talk tomorrow. We can agree on a time in the morning."

"Thank you, sir."

"At this point, then, our scene is over, and that's the end of our agreement for the evening. If we decide together to do this again, if one of us invites the other, then we would negotiate a new agreement."

"If one of us...I can ask you?"

"Of course you may." And wouldn't that be a miraculous evening?

"Huh." Nikki looked thoughtful. "And I still have to call you 'sir' when we leave here."

"Always. And keep your eyes respectfully low as well."

"Even when we're alone."

"Unless I instruct you otherwise, yes, *boy*." He emphasized the diminutive carefully.

"Yes, sir. Sorry, sir."

He stood and crossed the room to retrieve his jacket, letting the slip be just what it was and nothing more. "You should be proud of yourself, you did beautifully. I couldn't have asked for more."

Nikki smiled. "Thank you, sir."

"You may dress. I'm going to leave first, and then you can follow when you're ready. That will avoid the necessity for the kind of display I required you to put on earlier. Just leave when you please and get on with your evening any way you wish. I might suggest that you head straight home, first, because you need the rest, and second, because you are likely to be bombarded by questions if you decide to remain in the club."

"Oh. Yes, sir. I see what you mean, sir."

"I won't force another parade like that on you for a while. I am sorry that made you so uncomfortable. I hadn't realized you had that sort of performance anxiety."

"Neither did I, to be honest. Thank you, sir."

"We'll talk tomorrow, then. Good night, Nikki."

"Good night, sir."

13

Nikki twisted around, trying to get a better look at his shoulders in the bathroom mirror. God, they'd been so red Friday night, and now they looked totally fine. They weren't sore or rough or anything. His skin was soft from the lotion that Bradfo...Master Bradford had rubbed on for him a couple of times over the weekend.

Master Bradford. The only way he was going to get it right was to start thinking things like 'Sir' and 'Master' in his head. He wanted to get it right. He was still trying to make everything that happened fit in his mind somehow. He tried to think about it Friday night, but by the time he made it back to his room, he was so exhausted he just crashed. He'd been going over what he remembered in his mind all weekend long, and he was still preoccupied with it while he got ready for work this morning. He'd taken a long shower, shaved kind of needlessly, and was getting ready to get his harness on and get moving. He'd been trying, but in all that time, he still hadn't managed to find any clarity at all.

He knew a few things for sure. He'd enjoyed it and he wanted more. He trusted Bradford in a way he'd never trusted anyone in his life. And he finally felt like he might have found his tribe.

Maybe that was all the clarity he needed right now.

There was a knock at his door, and he hurried out of the bathroom.

"Nikki? Boy? May I come in?"

"Yes, sir," he answered with a smirk. He'd remembered.

The door opened and Bradford stepped right in, a worried look on his face. "Are you all right?"

Nikki shrugged. "Yes, sir. I'm fine."

Bradford looked him over. "You hadn't come looking for me yet and I was...concerned."

"I'm running a little late, sir. I'm sorry. I was just about to find you to ask for help with this."

Bradford seemed to relax. "Oh. Well, not to worry. The boss has excused any lateness this morning."

Wow, was that actually a joke? Nikki smiled. "He's a good boss, sir."

Bradford made a dismissive gesture. "Come here, boy, let's get that on you."

He went right over and handed Bradford the harness. He hadn't meant to worry anyone, but at the same time, it made him kind of happy to know that he had. That someone missed him, cared where he was. That was weird, right? He thought maybe it was weird.

Bradford settled the harness on his shoulders and did up the buckles, including the one on the back that he just couldn't reach for himself. The leather was starting to break in, and it was more and more comfortable every day.

"There you are." Bradford's hands slid over his shoulders.

He turned to face Master Bradford and gave him a smile. "Thank you, sir."

"You have stunning blue eyes, Nikki. They're captivating."

"I...uh." He wasn't sure what to make of the unexpected compliment. He felt his cheeks heat though....Was he blushing? "Thank you, sir."

"I'm surprised to be seeing them."

Oh, shit. He lowered his eyes to the floor. "I'm sorry, sir."

"It's quite all right, Nikki." Bradford laughed softly. "You will get used to it with practice."

"Am I supposed to avoid everyone's eyes, sir? Like Friday night?"

"Excellent question, boy. No. That was more about making things easier for you. Unless I tell you otherwise, you need only avoid the eyes of our Dominant members. And to be clear, that does not include Levi, despite his role as your supervisor. He is not a Dom."

"Yes, sir. Thank you, sir."

"You had better run along now, pup."

"Yes, sir. Have a good day, sir." He hurried from the room and grabbed a croissant from the bowl on Bradford's kitchen counter to inhale on his way to work.

On his way to work...which consisted of a walk down a long hallway and across the dining room. He laughed and swallowed the whole pastry down in three bites.

By the time he made it to the dining room, there was no one there. Nikki sighed, feeling really awful about being late, but Bradford said he'd been excused so he didn't worry about it much, just went looking for Levi and found him at the bar.

"Good morning, sir. I'm sorry I'm late."

Levi looked up from his paperwork. "You're excused this morning, Nikki, because you happen to have spent your weekend with Master Bradford and he called me. But a night with a Dom is not an excuse to show up late in the morning."

Nikki looked at Levi. "I'm sorry, sir."

"Cade is up on the second floor; you'll be working with him today. I am considering starting you on the schedule on your own next week. Do you think you'll be able to handle it?"

"Yes, sir. Definitely."

"Because if you're on your own, you can't be late."

"I have apologized for being late, sir. It won't happen again. Ask Chef. I was never late one day in the kitchen. This morning was—"

"I know."

Nikki sighed.

"Master Bradford said he was very proud of you. And I heard stories from Brian and Timothy about dinner."

Oh, God. Bradford wasn't kidding. People did talk. "I'll be on time, sir."

"I know you will."

"I'll go find Cade, sir."

"Listen, Nikki. Master Bradford doesn't throw around words like 'proud' very often, you know. He'll say pleased, intrigued, interested, satisfied...but proud is a rare thing for him to say. It sounds to me like you should also be proud of your work."

"Thank you, sir. It was an incredible experience." He wasn't sure what else to say. But he understood what Levi was telling him.

"Good. Off you go, then."

"Yes, sir." He hurried upstairs.

Cade had started off in the St. Andrews room as they had the other day, and it was weird going right back in there. He had a completely different response to it this morning after his evening with Master Bradford. Where before the room was intimidating but intriguing, now it felt comforting. It felt like he belonged here.

"Well, look who decided to come in finally." Cade looked at him, voice dripping with sarcasm.

"Oh, shut up. Brown-noser." He could give as good as he got.

"You're kind of a celebrity around here this morning." Cade flashed green eyes at him.

Nikki snorted. "Oh, great."

"It's all good, man. People are interested, that's all. They like you. You gonna go out with us tonight?"

"Out?"

"Sure. We all go out every Monday. The subs that don't have regular contracts, at least. It's fun."

"You know I'm not legal to drink, right?"

Cade snorted. "So have a Coke."

"You don't mind if I tag along?"

"You're not tagging along, Nikki, you're invited."

"Oh, but I—" He was about to tell Cade that he wasn't a sub again, but...he kind of thought he might be now. Maybe more than kind of. "Sounds like fun." Why not, right? He could go out and make some friends. That was what regular guys his age did, wasn't it? Go out. Have fun. He definitely could handle some fun.

He and Cade made quick work of the rest of the rooms. He figured he was making Cade crazy with all his questions, but Cade seemed pretty cool about them and didn't seem to mind. Nikki liked the idea that maybe he'd made a friend already.

After his shift, he went to his room to change. He pulled on jeans and a comfy T-shirt, then put some cash into the leather wallet Bradford had given him and stuffed it into his back pocket.

Cade had written down the address of the pub where everyone was meeting. It was a couple of blocks longer than what he usually thought of as walking distance, but Nikki went for it. It was a great night anyway; the summer air was really warm, and the streets were busy for a Monday night, full of people going here and there.

It took him a good half hour to get to the pub, and by the time he arrived he was thirsty. He ducked in through the heavy, wooden front doors and smiled. High tables, a long bar, lots of mahogany and glass, neon signs for Irish beer, and a soccer game on every TV. This place was awesome.

He headed inside, working his way along the bar and looking for the guys he was meeting. They found him first.

"Nikki, you made it!" He looked off to his left, and Brian was waving at him. He headed for the table, smiling at several familiar faces and shaking hands with Cade, Levi, Brian...and then greeting a bunch of guys he really didn't know at all.

Cade stood up for introductions. "Uh...let's see. You probably haven't met Garett and Kip..." He nodded to them. "And this is Rocky, and that's Noah." He was offered a chair between Brian and Noah. "What can I get you to drink?"

"Um. A Coke?"

Noah reached around him to get Brian's attention. "Hey, grab me another ginger ale while you're up, Bri?"

"Sure thing." Brian took off for the bar.

"So. You're Nikki."

Nikki looked at Noah and made a face. "Nope."

Noah laughed. "Yeah, I hear that."

"If I'd wanted to be a celebrity, I'd have moved to Hollywood."

"I remember that first walk across the dining room with Master Bradford. It's nerve-wracking. Everyone's watching you, wondering about the new sub that he's chosen, you feel like they're all judging you. It feels like the Doms are all scoping you out, the subs are sizing up the competition..."

Oh, wow. That was exactly it. It felt good to know he wasn't the only one that felt that way. "Totally. So, he does that with everyone?"

"Every new sub. It's like a rite of passage, you know? Master Bradford's way of letting everyone know that he's decided you're worth his time. Making sure the membership knows to take you seriously."

"Oh. Wow." *Worth his time...*

"They're not, though, you know."

"Not what?"

"They're not judging you."

He shrugged. *Right.* "I'm not sure I believe that."

"Honestly. I thought that myself but now that I've been on the other side, I get it. They're actually rooting for you. Hopeful. Welcoming. This group is really supportive."

"Yeah? Not all competitive?"

"It's not a race, Nikki."

"Huh." Those were words he was going to remember.

"One Coke, and one ginger ale." Brian set what looked like a Sprite down at his own spot.

"I thought I'd be the odd man out, not having a drink tonight."

"I don't drink," Noah said casually.

"I'm only twenty." Nikki laughed.

"Oh, good choice, then." Noah winked at him. "I'm a cop."

"Oh, my God."

Noah laughed. "I take it you had a good night with Bradford?"

"I...think so?"

"You want me to tell you how you know?" Noah picked up his ginger ale.

Now that was advice he could seriously use. "Tell me."

"It's not rocket science; it's actually really simple. Ask yourself, do you want more? Do you want to do it again? Try something else? If the answer is yes, then you had a good night. Works for everything. Even when you leave that room feeling off-center."

"That happens?"

"Not every scene is skewed toward you being satisfied when it's over, Nikki. Sometimes you're learning lessons, sometimes you cross boundaries you didn't know you had, sometimes things get emotional. Sometimes it's enough just to know you made your Dom happy, you know? You just need to know you did your best and hope that was enough for him. If you wake up in the morning still floating, it was a good night. If you wake up just feeling like you learned something, it was a good night. If you wake up in the morning feeling like a junkie that needs a fix, then it was definitely a good night." Noah laughed. "That's a gift I haven't had in a long while."

"Darts?" Rocky asked, laying a hand on Noah's shoulder.

"You're on, man." Noah stood up. "Do you want more? That's how you know, bottom line. Excuse me, Nikki."

"Oh. Yeah, sure. Thanks, Noah." Did he want more? Yeah. No question. So, it must have been a good night.

"So hey, you look good with clothes on." Cade grinned at Nikki, making him laugh.

"Yeah, right? You too."

"Cade!"

"Oh, Jamison just walked in. I'll be right back."

"Sure, okay." Nikki took a big sip of his Coke. That hit the spot.

"So? I'm dying to know." Brian said softly, leaning closer. "You have to tell me."

"Tell you...?"

"What you and Master Bradford did the other night!"

Oh, God. "It's okay if...I mean, I'm allowed to talk about it?" Was that right? It didn't feel entirely right.

Brian looked at him curiously. "Did he order you not to?"

"Well, no, but..."

Brian smiled, looking adorable but way too excited. "Cool. Then you can talk about anything you want."

"I'm kind of embarrassed, though. I mean, it won't be very interesting to someone that...well, like you I guess, that knows so much more than I do."

"Doesn't matter what you know, what matters is how you feel. Whether it was what you needed."

He looked at Brian. "Yeah?"

Brian nodded smiled. "It's okay if you don't want to talk about it, I understand. But if you have questions or something, I'm happy to help."

Questions. That was all he had. Even answers gave him more questions. Nikki shifted in his seat to face Brian. "We were in the St. Andrew's room."

"You like that one, huh? I heard you were curious about it. Cade told me Master Bradford interrupted you guys to show it to you."

"Yeah." The day that he completely lost it and Bradford helped him find...something else. Something better.

"So did he put you right on the cross?"

"No, no. He started me in the suspended cuffs, and he

just...tickled my shoulders with something."

"Oh, wow. I love that." Brian was the most honest person he'd ever met. Everything was just out there for people to see.

"I did too. And he did it, like, forever. Until everything tingled. After that he used a pinwheel, over and over. I don't even know how long because I kind of...I don't know."

"Drifted?"

"I guess?"

"Like you were floating? Kind of not on the ground? Not really in your head?"

That was it. "Yeah, like that. Then he moved me to the cross and..." He took a deep breath remembering the feeling of Bradford's paddle and the sound of his voice. "Wow."

Cade suddenly sat down in Noah's chair. "Did he fuck you?"

He looked at Cade sharply. "What? No." Had Cade been listening all this time?

"Shame."

"That wasn't part of our agreement."

"Ah. You drew a line at fucking."

"At sex."

"At all?" Cade looked horrified.

He didn't get it. So what if he didn't want sex with Bradford? "Yes."

Brian stared at him. "Wow, Nikki. I don't think any sub's ever done that to Master Bradford."

"Ever?" Nikki looked back at Brian, who shook his head. "Oh, come on."

"Not refusing any sex at all, no." Cade broke in again. "I mean Levi doesn't like paddles, but even he makes sure fucking is part of their agreement."

Nikki shrugged. He didn't have anything against sex. Sex

was great. He just...well, he wasn't ready for...sex with *Bradford*. Sex like *that*.

Sex with Cade on the other hand? Cade was fun.

"Wait. Are you not into men?" Brian asked.

Nikki snorted. "I'm into everybody."

Cade smiled at him. Nikki liked that smile.

"So, okay. What did he do, then?"

"He talked. A lot. And he...hit my ass with this padded paddle." A paddle. He'd let Bradford hit him with a paddle.

And he *liked* it.

"Ooh. Nice." Brian was listening intently.

"It went on forever."

Cade laughed. "It probably wasn't as long as you think."

"Whatever, it felt like forever."

Brian sighed. "He got you all floaty and pink."

"Way pink." *Wow.* His shoulders, his ass...it was amazing.

"You really are new."

"Did you like it?" Brian was asking the real questions.

He nodded. "I did. And he said he was proud of me."

Cade shifted in his seat. "Proud, huh?"

"Yeah. Levi said that was kind of a big deal."

"Well, pride in a Dom usually means they have some kind of attachment. They're teaching you something. Invested."

"Levi said something like that." Levi had said more, actually. He sipped his Coke and Cade took a big swig of whatever was in the cocktail glass the sub was holding.

"Well, damn, Nikki. Welcome to the club."

He hadn't joined the club. "I'm not paying dues, I'm not sure I'm..."

"Oh, you are." Cade tapped his knee "You don't pay dues until your trial period is over."

"When is it over?"

"When Master Bradford says it's over." Brian sounded very sure of that.

Nikki laughed. "That seems to be the answer to everything."

"It is." Cade and Brian laughed along with him, their eyes twinkling.

"Nikki, Nikki, Nikki."

Nikki looked up, finding Levi standing over him.

"Oh, boy." Cade stuck an elbow in Nikki's ribs and whispered, "Levi can get very, very drunk at these things."

"Nikki, you know you're Master Bradford's favorite right now, right?"

"What? Favorite?"

"He means favorite sub," Brian offered helpfully.

"You're a lucky, lucky man, Nikki."

"Oh, well. I mean, I'm just...new is all."

"How did he find you? I mean, you weren't a sub before you got here, right?"

"God, no," he said but realized immediately how that sounded. "I mean, I just didn't know what I was missing."

Cade laughed. "Good one."

"We met in a coffee shop, and he offered me the job in the kitchen."

Levi nodded. "That's amazing. Lucky you."

"Hey, Levi. You wanna go home?" Brian stood up and leaned into Levi.

"You coming with me?"

"I'll get you home, yeah."

Nikki watched Brian and Levi go, and Cade leaned back in his chair. "Brian doesn't really like these get-togethers much; they're not his thing. But he comes every week anyway."

"Because of Levi?"

Cade nodded. "Yep. To make sure Levi gets home okay. He's been doing it for like a year."

"Why?"

"No idea. Maybe they're sleeping together."

He nodded. Maybe. Or maybe it was just who Brian was. Levi obviously had something going on if he got blasted every week.

"Garett and Kip will head out together shortly, too."

"Yeah? Noah and Rocky?"

Cade laughed. "No. Oh, no. Not Noah."

"He's really a cop?"

"Yeah, but it doesn't have anything to do with that. He just...doesn't."

"Really? Why?"

"He doesn't sleep around. Or so he says. Wants to save it for the Doms."

"Hm." Nikki looked at Noah. He could respect that. But Noah was a good-looking man. That must drive at least some of these guys crazy.

"You and Rocky?"

Cade shook his head. "Nope."

"You and anybody?"

Cade leaned in closer. "Nope."

"Oh." He leaned toward Cade too. "Good."

"Sure is."

Cade kissed him, and he returned it, grinning against Cade's lips. This could be fun. "Are you drunk?"

"Maybe a little. Sure you don't want a beer?"

"Is the cop still around?"

"Nope."

"Bring it on."

"Be right back."

14

Bradford had hoped that Nikki might join him for dinner, but he'd found a note on his kitchen counter from the boy:

Going out tonight.

Of course. He ought to have assumed—now that Nikki was officially one of the uncontracted subs—that he would be invited out for their Monday night gatherings. Bradford technically wasn't supposed to know about the regular meet-up, but when it came to his members, very little got past him. He was privy to virtually all the gossip, both in and outside the club. No, the boys' regular Monday meeting was no secret to him, but outside of the club he had no jurisdiction over how they spent their time, and in all the years the tradition had been in place, he'd never heard of anything untoward going on, and only very few, minor cases of heartbreak.

Boys will be boys, eh? Besides, it wasn't a bad thing for them to be fond of each other.

However, that left him to his own devices. He'd been busy through the weekend but had hoped to further discuss their evening together with Nikki over dinner tonight. Now he felt at loose ends. He sat in his favorite chair in his study, a crystal decanter on the table beside him, a glass of cognac warming in one hand, and a cigarette burning in the other.

In the deafening silence, he found himself second-guessing everything. He had no rational cause for concern. The evening with Nikki had gone just perfectly as far as he could tell, but he needed to talk to the boy. He needed to hear Nikki tell him it was okay, that it was a good experience.

What Bradford really needed was for Nikki to agree to do it again, to say that he wanted more.

Dammit.

He took a drag of his cigarette and washed it down with a sip of his cognac. Nikki was so similar to the young man he had once been. Broke, homeless, wishing for something easier. The big difference was that even at the young age of twenty, Bradford had been longing *for* control, whereas Nikki was longing to relinquish it.

Ah, Harrison. Am I doing right by this boy?

It was important to him that he was reading and following Nikki's cues and not merely seducing the boy into a life he would not have otherwise wanted.

Then again, if the boy is happy, does it matter?

He'd been well aware of his own proclivities before Harrison took him in. He'd been the Dominant partner in every sexual encounter he'd ever had, and he'd started quite young. His first sexual experience had been as frightening as it was enlightening, with the simple truth of losing his virginity far less remarkable to him than the way he'd used his partner. It fell short of truly hurting the boy, and he'd backed off the moment he was asked, but at first his hunger terrified him. His partner was more experienced, quite understanding, and their discussion afterward might literally have saved him from himself. All the same, he learned to be very open with new lovers and insisted on full consent because he knew he could be rough: pinning wrists, smacking and bruising, using his body weight, employing words and the tone of his voice to manipulate.

Little had changed in that department.

By eighteen years old he could barely afford to eat, but he owned a set of leather cuffs and a short-handled flogger. His nature and his needs were very clear to him.

It was Harrison that molded him into the Dom he had since become however, alongside a number of very focused and competitive contemporaries such as Tobias and Luca. The first thing Harrison did was forbid Bradford any sex play at all in his scenes, in an effort to illustrate the divide between the art and the need. Being young, still in his midtwenties, the two had been inseparable in his mind; the purpose of the whip and the cuffs was to get someone excited, to get them off—to get himself off.

Harrison taught him the higher purpose of their craft. Through that deprivation and Harrison's passion for the lifestyle, he was able to separate his needs from his desires and learn what was at the root of each.

He snuffed his cigarette and stared out the window at the busy city streets, swirling the last sip of cognac.

———

Nikki and Cade went barreling through Cade's front door, and it slammed behind them.

Maybe it was the beer. Maybe it was all that talk about his scene with Bradford. Or about fucking Bradford.

Maybe just because Cade was hot and being so nice to him.

"Hey, man."

Nikki felt the other sub wave one of his roommates off as he shoved his tongue down Nikki's throat again.

"Whoa, gotcha. I was just going to hit the bar."

"Was that Cade?"

"And...someone."

"Woohoo! You go, man!" Someone cheered from another room.

"Come on, Jackie, let's get out of here."

"Yep. Just finding my shoes."

Cade caught his eye. "They're going."

"Okay." Nikki was breathless and just barely managed to get the word out. Cade pressed him up against the wall in the hallway and ground a stiff erection into his thigh. "Shit, I feel that, man."

"Yeah." Cade grunted.

Nikki shifted and rubbed right back, both of them finding friction. He moaned. "Want your mouth."

"Later, gentlemen!" Cade's roommates were laughing as they took off through the front door, and he heard the dead bolt click home.

Cade reached up and pulled his shirt off over his head. "Come on." Cade pulled him by the hand, hurrying down the hall to a small bedroom. There was a twin bed and a window that looked into an alley with a view of a brick wall not three feet away. Cade closed the door behind them. "You top? I have rubbers."

"No, you?"

Cade laughed. "Hell, no."

He pulled off his T-shirt. "No problem. Sixty-nine?"

"Oh, fun!" Cade grinned wide and tossed his jeans aside.

Fun was exactly what he was looking for. He watched Cade, who was hard as hell.

Cade actually hissed as he maneuvered his jeans down around his erection. He grinned at Nikki and wrapped his fingers around his own shaft, grunting as he gave it a tug. "This bad boy needs some love."

Nikki dropped his jeans too, laughing. "Let me see what I can do for you." He kicked all his clothing aside and reached out, shooing Cade's fingers away and replacing them with his own. Cade moaned for him and his eyes slid closed. "Oh, wow, Cade. I totally see what the Doms like about you."

"Shut up. And don't stop." Cade's voice had dropped to a whisper and his lips parted slightly as Nikki stroked him. He really was beautiful. Nikki leaned forward and kissed him, and Cade's fingers reached up and wrapped around Nikki's nape.

"Want," he whispered back.

"Come on." Cade led Nikki to his tiny bed.

———

Bradford sat across from Harrison in one of the wingback library chairs and sipped his brandy. "This is pretty good."

"Delightful. Marvelous. Luscious."

Bradford laughed. "What was all of that?"

Harrison smiled at him. "A short list of more sophisticated descriptive words you might have substituted for 'pretty good.'"

"What's wrong with 'pretty good'?"

"It doesn't say anything, Bradford. It's an empty phrase. A waste of words. And it makes you sound rather like the guttersnipe you were when I first brought you home."

"Now you're just being an asshole, Harry." Bradford sighed.

He'd been working on his turn of phrase and his presentation as part of his training. Harrison had insisted on it. "I am the guttersnipe you brought home. I just smell better."

Harrison laughed softly and stood, setting his brandy down on the table between them. "Heavens no, Bradford, you most certainly are not. On the contrary, you have become a true Dominant. You appreciate the art in the balance of personal power, and you're easily one of the most competent and capable students I've ever had. You simply have been disadvantaged by the circumstances that surrounded your youth."

"Circumstances." Bradford snorted. "You mean being kicked out...ah." Bradford slowed down and chose his words more carefully. "Being evicted from my parents' home at the tender age of fourteen?"

"Now, that was very nice."

Bradford shook his head at Harrison and went on. "Or perhaps you mean being penniless, sleeping in shelters and alleys or on park benches? Don't be such a snob, Harry."

"I don't mean any of those things, Bradford. I'm talking about your lack of consistent education."

Bradford sighed. "I did the best I could."

Harrison walked around behind Bradford's chair. "What you were able to do was remarkable. Your ambition has served you well." Harrison leaned on the back of the chair, his voice low in Bradford's ear. "You're brilliant, Bradford. I want you to understand that. You're not traditionally educated, it's true, yet you've absorbed everything you needed to know. All you require now is a little polish, and you will be fully capable of running my business. It is my sincere hope that you will one day."

"What? Me?"

"That's what I'm offering you, Dear One."

Bradford stood up and walked around his chair, so he was standing in front of his mentor.

His mentor, his lover.

He'd never pictured himself in a May-December relationship —or any relationship—and yet... "Spell this out for me, Harry. I need to make sure I'm hearing you right."

"Stay with me, Bradford." Harrison took both of Bradford's hands in his. "After your training is finished. Live with me, here in my brownstone."

"Harrison." Bradford's heart was beating hard.

"I'm not getting any younger. I have to leave all of this to someone—the house, my estate, the club and its assets. Stay with me, be my friend, my lover. Everything you are now only...until death do us part."

Harrison's words took Bradford's breath away. "You're asking me to marry you?"

"Quietly, dearest. Privately, but yes. A gentleman's agreement, just between us. I'm asking for a promise, a pledge if you will, to take care of me, whatever the future may bring. I can't imagine having to live out my third act alone. In return, I will leave you everything."

Bradford raised an eyebrow, trying to ignore the hollow ache Harrison's words left in his chest. "I see. So, it's really more of a business arrangement, then."

"No, Dear One." Harrison reached up and combed a lock of Bradford's hair off his forehead with gentle fingers. "Well, partly it has to be, I suppose. But it's so much more. It's only that—"

"You have a reputation." That much Bradford understood. "And being lovers with another Dom doesn't serve your image."

Harrison's smile was sad but affectionate. "I'm sorry. It's weak and selfish of me, I know. But it's what I need." Harrison sank to one knee, keeping those worn but wise hazel eyes locked on Bradford's and a tight hold on Bradford's fingers. "My Heart, it doesn't diminish the way I feel about you."

———

Bradford ran his fingers through his hair and tossed back the last sip of his cognac. He had been Harrison's whole heart, he knew, right up until the day it stopped beating. He loved Harrison still—quietly, privately, as his lover had intended. In all their years together, they never attended a party as a couple, never held hands in public, never kissed one another outside of the brownstone. Of course, there were a handful of their inner circle who knew, people like Tobias for one, and he had to believe that the word got out among the senior club members prior to Harrison's memorial at the club, because no one seemed to question the extent of his grief. If that was the case, though, everyone had respected his privacy.

There was no question that the club was the second love of his life and he'd poured himself into it, knowing that keeping it whole, keeping the membership vibrant and varied, keeping it a safe and supportive environment for men with certain shared interests would make Harrison proud. He'd added his own touches, of course. For example, his lover hadn't ever been the extrovert that Bradford was at heart and had never been as fond of parties and entertaining as he was.

Speaking of parties, his birthday was right around the corner. Planning was something he could do instead of sitting alone in the library feeling sorry for himself.

15

He probably should feel guilty or something about staying out all night. He probably should be ready to apologize to Bradford for not calling to let him know. He probably shouldn't have had that beer.

But fuck it, he'd had so much fun.

Nikki headed down the hall toward the club, in jeans and a T-shirt. Bradford's dinner invitation didn't really leave room to turn him down:

Dinner, 7:00pm. Wear whatever you like, boy. If I have my way, you won't be wearing it long.

He shivered and the note fluttered in his fingers.

If I have my way.

Bradford was pretty used to getting his way.

He stepped into the dining room and looked around.

"Hi, Nikki." Brian came out of nowhere, making him jump.

"Jesus, Brian."

Brian just grinned at him. "Sir is over in the corner there; he said he wanted a more private table. Would you like me to walk with you?"

He was relieved. He'd rather not be out in the middle of everything. God, that was nerve-wracking. He followed Brian to the table, still trying to decide how to present himself. Contrite and apologetic? Confident and cheerful? Apologetic and cheerful? *Damn.*

"Good evening, boy."

"Hello, sir." He kept his eyes low but his voice steady. "Thank you for the dinner invitation." There. That was polite.

"I'm glad you could join me. Did you have a pleasant evening?"

There was more than a hint of amusement in Bradford's tone. Was that a trick question? "Yes, sir."

"Good thing you had the day off today."

"Yes, sir." Good thing, for sure.

This conversation was surreal.

"I hope my choice of seating will ease your performance anxiety, boy, but you will be honest with me if you find it difficult, won't you?"

"Yes, sir. Thank you, sir." It was cool of Bradford to think of that. It was really hard to relax out in the middle of everything and everyone.

"Good. Please, have a seat."

Brian had been waiting patiently behind him and on Bradford's order, pulled out his chair for him. "Thanks." He looked at Brian and gave him an awkward smile. It was still odd to be friends one day and to have Brian or Levi or whoever serving the next.

"Your note was...direct, sir."

"This is a negotiation. I want what I want. It doesn't serve either of us to mince words."

"Well, no, but—"

"Unless you're telling me you're not interested."

"No, sir. Uh. I mean yes, sir. Or...no, sir, I'm not *not* interested." Jesus. Why was he so flustered?

Bradford grinned at him patiently and said absolutely nothing.

He took a second to breathe and tried again. "Sorry, sir. I would be honored to serve you this evening."

"Thank you, boy. I am pleased."

He wished he understood why he was blushing. He didn't care really that he had—he just didn't know why. "Thank you, sir."

"The sub plate for you, then?"

"Whatever you think is best, sir."

He heard Bradford's breath catch, and he looked up as high as Bradford's chin, hoping to get a look at the Dom's face and understand what that sound meant. Seemed like the more he wanted to know, the less he understood.

"You really are a treasure, boy."

"I...I'm sure I'm not, sir. But thank you."

"Hm. We'll work on that." Bradford leaned back in his chair. "Brian, small plate for Nikki and I'll have the Cobb salad please, and I'd like a nice hunk of bread with that. Ask Chef, he'll know what I mean."

"Yes, sir." He watched Brian carefully pour out water for each of them, his friend moving gracefully but maybe in too much of a hurry.

Brian gave a little nod to Bradford.

"Run along, boy."

"Yes, sir." Brian disappeared.

He smiled, imagining that Road Runner puff of smoke behind Brian's heels.

"I am pleased to learn that you want to sub for me again, boy. We haven't spoken about the other night and although I thought it went well for you, it would be nice to hear how the experience sat with you firsthand."

Jesus, couldn't the man just ask if he liked it? All this flowery language was so...well, okay, it was so *Bradford*. Maybe he didn't want to change it after all. "It was intense. I surprised myself a little. You surprised me a lot. It was a good experience, but I don't have...I can't really sum it up neatly."

Bradford had been listening closely. "That's fine. You will in time, I'll help you. But for now, it's enough for me to know you felt it was a good experience. I am looking forward to exploring with you. Taking you further, staying there longer."

He nodded. "I want that. I mean, I'd like that, sir."

"Excellent. But I want more this time, Nikki." Bradford's tone was smooth and direct.

What the heck did that mean? "More, sir?"

"More than a scene. More than just tonight. I want a full day. Two if you're willing."

"Two days?" He honestly wasn't sure what that meant.

"Yes, Nikki. Two days. A very short contract, if you will. Two days of consistent, continual submission."

Two days? He had questions. "So, we'd do a scene and...?"

"Your responsibility to me, and mine to you of course, wouldn't end there. We would continue for forty-eight hours, or thereabouts."

"With me as your sub. Full on. For two days." How the hell did that work?

"Exactly. Yes. Barring the use of your safe words of course."

"I could use my safe words any time?"

"Yes."

"Even when we're not in a scene?"

"Any time at all, if you feel you need them. They are your words, Nikki, darling, and I will honor them always."

Wow. So, two days of...well, belonging to Bradford, basically. "What about work?"

Bradford smiled at him. "I would arrange for you to have the time off."

"Oh. Well yeah, you are the boss, I guess."

"Just so."

Duh. He could be such an idiot sometimes. "Well, I mean, I guess if I can still use my words, I don't see why not."

Bradford leaned forward. "Boy?"

The way Bradford said that word was so intense, it sent a shiver up his spine. "Yes, sir?"

"Do you want to be mine for two days?"

"Well, I—"

"Mine, Nikki. To hit, to hurt, to teach, to uplift, to praise, to bend to my will for forty-eight hours?"

His mouth went dry and all he could do was nod. *Jesus.* Those words were hot. Seductive.

"I suppose your rules are still in place?"

His rules. *Think, Nikki.* "My—"

"No sex?"

"Oh! Oh. Yes. No sex." Bradford could definitely turn him on, but Nikki still didn't feel like he understood. Was it just a scene thing? Did it make everything more...real? Was there anything more real? It felt like sex should have some kind of meaning attached to it in a scene, and he needed to figure everything out first.

Bradford nodded slowly, looking thoughtful. "I respectfully request a negotiation."

"Negotiation?" *What?* That was weird.

"Well, it is a contract meant to meet both of our needs, so I'd like to propose a compromise."

"How...how do you compromise about sex?"

He thought he might have seen a hint of a smile on Bradford's lips for a moment, but it was gone so quickly, he couldn't be sure. "I'll agree to no penetration, no oral, no fondling of your intimate places. But Nikki, I'd like your permission to touch you in-scene. Your skin. Your body. I'd like permission to soothe, to caress, to give you the warmth of my hands. Not just in reassurance as I have been, but in earnest. Because I want to."

He swallowed back a rising lump in his throat. "To...give me...?"

"Yes, a gift. To support and to comfort you, and to satisfy me."

He thought about that. "I have my words." He wasn't sure if he was trying to remind Bradford or himself.

"Always."

Nikki's nod came easily enough. He liked the trust between them. "All right."

"And what about pain?"

Right. He'd had a rule about that, too. But he'd liked Bradford's paddle and he already knew he wanted to try more. Just to try. "Can you...take it slow?"

"I can and I will. That's usually the best way, Nikki, darling."

He nodded. "Then we...you can try some." He had butterflies in his stomach all of a sudden. But he wasn't afraid, or even nervous really. He was...excited? Anxious to get started.

When Brian finally returned with their dinner, he put his hand up, refusing the plate. "I better not."

Bradford nodded to Brian and the plate disappeared.

"Have some water, boy. At least."

He nodded and sipped his water slowly while Bradford ate. The man was taking his time and it was maddening. He wanted to get started. Finally, Bradford put his fork down. "Ordinarily, boy, at this point I would have you get up and kneel by me for a few minutes to find your headspace before we headed upstairs. I am willing to alter that routine so that you don't feel uncomfortable."

He smiled; Bradford's thoughtfulness was meaningful to him. "Thank you, sir."

"Not forever, boy. For now."

"Yes, sir. Thank you, sir."

"Good boy." Bradford nodded to him. "You really are learning quickly." Bradford took a sip of his water. "So. You will get up and go straight upstairs to the St. Andrews room, hm? You can take whatever route you prefer. If you don't want to cross the dining room, you are welcome to go back through the brownstone and in the front door to the club, or even cut through the kitchen, whatever suits you. I'll be up in ten minutes. When you get there, use the restroom. Then strip and leave your clothing in a neat pile by the door, and kneel in the center of the room. Don't let your mind wander. Think about how you will please me this evening. How you will serve me tomorrow. Prepare." Bradford handed him a key. "For the St. Andrew's Room."

Whoa.

He blinked at Bradford for a second. Use the restroom, strip, prepare...that was all pretty specific.

"Something wrong, boy? Do you need clarification?"

"Oh. Uh. No, sir."

"Go along, then."

"Yes, sir." He popped up out of his seat, took the key, and headed back into the house.

16

Two days.

The boy had agreed to two days without hesitation. Nikki knew the meaning of those safe words, the comfort it gave a sub, even if the boy didn't completely comprehend yet the control it gave him. It was a constant wonder how few subs truly grasped the influence inherent in their safe words: the power it gave a sub who so willingly relinquished himself.

It was all he could do to stay in his seat for those ten long minutes. He felt like a child who'd been told he had to wait to open a gift.

Two days. A nice long scene tonight, a good night's sleep at the foot of his bed, a boy to kneel at his feet tomorrow in his office just because he wanted Nikki there. Oh, it had been a long while since he'd done this for himself.

And Nikki would get a taste of what he could have if he wanted it. It would certainly be an enlightening discussion in the days to come.

He had such plans for this session: pain and reward, subtle hints at seduction, a test of endurance, all in the hopes of finding a boundary to push. Something for Nikki to discover and conquer, no matter how small.

He stood finally and Brian appeared at his side to pull out his chair and help him on with his jacket. "Thank you, boy."

"Enjoy your evening, sir."

"Thank you, pup. You, too."

He made his way slowly across the dining room, shaking hands and greeting men along the way as usual. The club was busy tonight, and he was glad to see it. It was meant to be busy, meant to be bustling with men who understood each other. A safe place for everyone to be who they were without judgment.

As he ascended the stairs, he took a moment to get his head right. Who he was when he walked through that door was so important, it would set the tone for the evening. He took a deep breath before using a second key and stepping into the room.

Nikki was kneeling as he'd asked, naked, clothes folded, everything just as he'd requested. But the boy looked up sharply as he entered the room.

"Eyes down, boy."

Nikki looked down quickly. "You startled me, sir."

"Then you were not in the right headspace. Tell me what you were thinking about."

"I...uh. I'm not sure, sir."

"I gave you specific instructions, boy." Oh, this was going to be marvelous. He took off his coat and hung it in the small closet.

"Yes, sir. And I did think about it, sir."

"Did I not expressly tell you not to let your mind wander?"

"But I—"

"Boy! What did I tell you?" He barked.

Nikki flinched and shifted on his knees. "To think about how I would please you."

"Do I sound pleased?"

"No, sir."

"No." He rolled up his sleeves slowly, his actions far more relaxed than his words. "Crawl to me, boy, and apologize."

"Wait. Crawl?"

Oh-ho. Could this evening's lesson present itself more quickly or more clearly?

"Whelp." He said it smoothly. There was nothing to be gained by anger if Nikki didn't understand what he'd done wrong. "Now you may crawl over to that wall and retrieve the paddle we used the other night."

The boy sighed, but he started to move toward the wall.

"An acknowledgment is appropriate, boy."

"Oh! Yes, sir. I'm sorry, sir."

"So many apologies. You'll understand better in a moment."

Nikki stood up and took the paddle off the wall, then dropped back to his knees and crawled over to him with it. "Very nice, boy. Your instinct was excellent there." He considered ordering the boy to carry the paddle with those lovely white teeth, but he felt that might be taking his point further than necessary.

This time.

When Nikki stopped in front of him, Bradford reached down and took the paddle. He ran his hand along Nikki's jaw and cheek as he spoke. "Nothing I do is for its own sake, Nikki. I won't ask you to crawl just to see you crawl. I won't order you to lick my boots just because I can. Some Doms might, and it's my right of course, but that's not my style. If I choose to make a request you might find humiliating, there is purpose for it. Whether it's a lesson to be learned, a headspace I need you in, a punishment, reward, or reminder, there will always be a reason."

Nikki listened, still and silent on his hands and knees.

"Drop to your forearms. If you're not sure what I mean, you may ask."

Nikki shifted so that his elbows were on the floor, and his hands and forearms as well. "Like this, sir?"

"Like that. Very nice, boy." He walked around behind Nikki and gave his ass a light tap with the paddle. "Sometimes I will warn you when I plan to strike you and sometimes I won't. If I have a paddle in my hand, I think it's a fair assumption that I plan to use it, hm?" Another tap to Nikki's other bare ass cheek.

"Yes, sir."

"This position you are in offers me your ass to do as I please." He paced behind Nikki as he spoke. "I can hit you, I can touch you, I could fondle you or fuck you, were those things in our agreement. I could plant a heavy-soled boot on one of your lovely pale cheeks, my boy. Do you understand?"

"Yes...sir?"

"Was that a question?"

"Yes, sir."

"Ask it."

"Am I being punished, sir?"

"Ah. Excellent question." Bradford tapped each cheek lightly again. "No, boy. You're being instructed not to question my orders. The next time you do so you will be punished, however."

Nikki nodded. "Yes, sir."

Bradford went a little harder and the paddle made a

satisfying thud as it landed on Nikki's ass. "The purpose of a paddle of this sort is to help you find your headspace. Concentrate on it and my voice, feel it warm your body and calm your mind." He began to paddle again, not hard at all but rhythmic, stroke after stroke, the dull thud of the paddle against bare skin filling the room. He didn't stop this time as he spoke. "When you are in the right space, there will be nothing in this room but me and you."

Thud. Thud. Thud. Thud. Relentless.

"My paddle and your body."

Thud. Thud. Monotonous in its repetition.

"My voice and your breathing."

Nikki grunted softly and he picked up the pace, adding a bit more strength in his arm. For a long while, he said nothing. He continued until Nikki's grunts had turned to soft moans, the boy's ass was red, and Bradford's arm began to tire. He backed off, first the strength of his blows and then the pace, returning to the slow, light taps with which he'd begun.

He felt warm himself and found that he had relaxed more fully into his own headspace. He watched Nikki, motionless and breathing deeply, and decided that this was an excellent way to settle them both. He might just keep it in their routine.

He paced the room and put the paddle away to be cleaned, then took off his jacket and hung it in the closet. Nikki didn't move or say a word.

"Boy."

"...sir."

"Sit up now, boy. You've done very well."

"Thank you, sir." Nikki sat up slowly, settling onto his heels tentatively at first, but he seemed to realize quickly

140JODI PAYNE

that Bradford hadn't damaged him, or even hurt him enough to worry about a sting. "I feel much better, sir."

He had been about to ask Nikki how things felt, but the boy just offered a much bigger answer to him, like a gift. He felt the thrill of success in his spine, but he tucked his joy away for later and kept his voice even for Nikki, to help the boy hold on to that headspace. "I am gratified to hear that. Were you feeling nervous before?"

"Yes, sir. Anxious, I think. Impatient. But now I...I feel..."

"Calm?"

"Yes, sir. I do."

Well, wasn't that remarkable? Again, he was convinced that Nikki needed this lifestyle. The boy took to it so naturally. Every time he worried that perhaps he was manipulating the boy, or forcing something that wasn't there, every time he wondered if he was doing the right thing, Nikki would prove to him that he was. This time, without prompting of any kind, the boy not only found his center but he understood that Bradford had taken him there.

Center was a wonderful start, but subspace was something else. Subspace was the goal.

"Stand up, boy." Nikki stood and he made a slow circle around his sub. The boy's eyes were low. "Clasp your hands behind you." When Nikki complied, he manipulated them a bit, lining up the boy's hands with the small of his back. "Straighten your shoulders, spread your feet a bit wider. Good. Very good." He moved in front of Nikki again. "Who are you, boy?"

"I am your sub, sir."

"Yes. Good boy. So you are. How does doing what I ask and earning praise from your Master make you feel?"

"I...it makes me feel...it feels good to know I've done well, sir. It makes me happy. Proud."

Bradford smiled. "Then lift your chin, boy. Show me that being my sub and earning my praise makes you proud."

Nikki did as he asked and the image was complete, the boy's stance picture-perfect. Beautiful.

"Excellent. This is what I will call 'display,' Nikki. If I ask you to display, this is what I expect to see. If I ask for a kneeling display, it will be just the same but on your knees. Do you understand?"

"Yes, sir."

"Take a moment to be sure you know how it feels; then walk to the cross and face it in display, please."

Bradford waited patiently while Nikki paused, looking thoughtful, and then slowly moved over to the cross and settled into a lovely display position. He took a moment to admire Nikki's back and shoulders, the boy's thighs, and considered the various instruments he could use next. He left them all in their places for the time being and stepped close to Nikki. "Place your hands up on the cross, and get your feet into position," he whispered into the boy's ear.

Bradford bound the boy in slowly, taking his time and caressing each leg and arm carefully, deliberately, with long strokes from torso to fingers and toes. He noticed Nikki's breathing pick up slightly and tension creep into the boy's shoulders. "Relax, boy. You are safe. I will take care of you. And you have your words. Give them to me again, now."

"Nickel and dime, sir."

" 'Nickel and dime' are your words. As a refresher, boy, if you say 'nickel' I will stop what I am doing and ask you what you need before proceeding or changing things up. If you say 'dime,' then the scene will end immediately. I will free your hands and feet and we will talk over what happened. Is that acceptable?"

"Yes, sir. Thank you, sir."

"Do not be afraid to use them if you need to. I will not be upset or disappointed with you. And say them with conviction. Make sure I can hear you. Understood?"

"Yes. Thank you, sir."

The more he reassured Nikki of his safety, the more he watched the boy's shoulders relax. "Are you comfortable now, boy? Anything too tight?"

Nikki didn't answer right away, testing the bonds and resettling his feet. "I'm fine, sir."

Satisfied, Bradford walked over to the wall and examined the floggers that hung there, looking for one with more bark than bite. His fingers itched for the shot loaded, oiled leather flogger that was his tool of choice with an experienced sub— oh, the things he could do to the boy's lovely canvas of pale skin with that instrument—but it was far too intense for Nikki yet. Instead he pulled down a suede flogger with wide falls, going for a decent thud coupled with only a very light sting.

He tested it in the air a few times, then on the divan, against his own thigh. "I've got a flogger, boy." He walked around in front of the free-standing cross so he could show it to Nikki. "Have a look at it. There are about forty falls made of suede, so it will have a decent weight and make a lovely thudding sound against your skin, but it won't sting much. This one is fancy, meaning it's been balanced by this silver ring on the end of the handle. That gives me more control, I can be quite precise with my placement."

Nikki watched closely as he pointed out the different parts of the flogger.

"So, before you ask, yes, I'm going to use it. And yes, I

will start slow as I promised. Do you have other questions, boy?"

"Can I touch it?"

Bradford smiled. "Later. After we're done." He let Nikki believe that was because his hands were restrained, but it was more than that. Anticipation of the unknown was a lovely tool, if short-lived. "We will begin, hm? Remember your words," he said once more as he moved out of Nikki's line of sight.

"Yes, sir."

He drew the flogger up the outside of Nikki's leg and across his ass, letting the falls drag against the boy's skin. A moment later he began to swing the falls underhanded against Nikki's calves and thighs.

"So, boy. You didn't come back to the brownstone last night."

"No, sir."

"I'm glad you had a good evening. But in the future, a phone call would be appropriate, boy. So I know not to expect you."

"Yes, sir. I'm sorry, sir. I...lost track of time."

"I can understand how that might happen. Still...next time."

"Yes, sir."

Bradford switched to an overhand strike, very light, barely more than a flick of his wrist, the falls tapping gently against Nikki's shoulders. "Who were you with?"

"Sir?"

"Did you not understand the question, boy?" He laid one slightly more intense strike and then returned to sensation only.

"I understood, sir, I—"

"If you don't want to answer my question, you are welcome to use your words, boy."

"Cade," Nikki said quickly. "I stayed with Cade."

Bradford played with him. "Really? He's lovely, isn't he? Slept on the couch, did you?"

"No, sir. I slept in his bed."

"Oh, and he slept on the couch."

"No, sir. We slept together in his bed."

"You slept together? Or you *slept* together?"

"I...sir, I—"

He took a step back so he could strike with the full extension of his arm. The blows grew consistent and heavier. "Answer the question or use your words, boy."

"Just blowjobs, sir."

He grinned. Cade and fellatio went together like fish and chips. "Very nice. Cade has a masterful mouth, doesn't he?"

"He...sir?"

"What is it, boy?" he asked with a laugh. "Do you imagine Cade would be insulted by my praise? I assure you I have told him as much myself."

"I suppose not, sir."

Bradford landed a set of blows to the flat wide area of Nikki's shoulders, four in a row, half-power. Nikki gasped. "Did you like his mouth on you?"

The boy nodded. "Yes, sir."

He started raining blows down on Nikki's skin. First the boy's shoulders, then those pale thighs, then back again. It wasn't long before Nikki's shoulders fell and the hands that had been balled into fists relaxed and flattened against the cross.

But when Nikki moaned and that head of blond hair bent forward, he knew the boy was his. "Good, boy."

Now he could have what he needed.

The next set of blows were full-power, aimed precisely for the center of each of Nikki's already pinked ass cheeks.

"Ah!" Nikki cried out. "Sir!"

"I'm listening. Use your words if you need them, boy."

But Nikki didn't. The boy stayed silent.

Trusting in the very light sting of the flogger and his boy's understanding of safe words, he let fly, using his whole arm, skillfully battering the wide expanses of skin on Nikki's back, ass, and thighs. He was watchful, of course, as he would be with any sub, and though Nikki grunted for him, the boy never once shied away from his flogger. It wasn't until Nikki was breathing fairly heavily that Bradford slowed the blows, lightened up, and finally halted them altogether.

"Still with me, boy?"

"Yes, sir." Nikki's voice was a great deal stronger than he would have expected.

"How do you feel?"

"Fine, sir. Relaxed."

Relaxed. Settled. And quite coherent. "Are you feeling sore? Tired?"

"No, sir. I want more."

"More?" He could hardly believe what he was hearing.

"It's not enough, I...please, sir. I need more."

"More strokes?"

"Well, yes but more...I want to *feel* more."

Feel more.

He looked at the flogger in his hands. It was a heavy fall but mild on the skin. The boy wanted more sting. He was feeling plenty warmed up, so he tossed that flogger over with the paddle and reached for the next level up, a fancy combo flogger with twenty falls. This one was still half suede, but it was half oiled leather and would give Nikki a pretty good introduction to what the boy was asking for. He also grabbed a bottle of water and brought it to the boy.

"Water," he said, offering it to Nikki who nodded. He held the bottle while Nikki drank deep. "This one is thinner, and half of its tails are leather. You let me know how you like it. Hm?"

"Yes, sir. Thank you, sir."

"You might not want to thank me yet, boy." But something about Nikki's demeanor suggested that the boy was more than ready. He ran a hand over Nikki's back. The skin was pink and well-warmed by the suede flogger, but there were no marks or lines from the individual strands of leather. That would change shortly.

"All right, boy. Because I've found a new flogger at your request, you will thank me again each and every time I pause."

"Yes, sir."

"And remember your words." Bradford didn't hesitate and laid two full-out strokes in succession across Nikki's ass.

Nikki hissed and he watched the boy's toes curl. "Fuck."

"Swear if you must boy. Say anything you like, but thank me for it."

"Sorry. Thank you, sir."

Bradford laid four more across the sub's shoulders, heavy blows placed carefully so he could repeat them precisely. As he pulled his arm back, Nikki thanked him, sounding a bit breathless. He paused a moment longer, but the boy didn't have anything more to say this time, so Bradford raised his arm. The boy wanted more, had his words, and so far didn't seem to be anywhere near them.

And this was starting to feel good.

He landed four more blows directly on top of the ones

he'd just laid on Nikki's shoulders, and then without pause, he added four to his sub's ass as well.

"Thank you, sir!" Nikki ground out between gritted teeth. "Thank you."

He wanted to take Nikki in a bit, stall so he could be sure the boy was all right. "How do you feel, boy?"

"Good, sir. So good."

"Enough?"

"No, sir. I'm fine, sir."

If Nikki was fine, he had some work to do. "You want more?"

"Yes, sir."

"Beg."

"Beg, sir?"

"Yes, boy. If you want it, beg for it."

"Please, sir?" He had to smile at the boy's enthusiasm and the lack of hesitation in following his command. "Can I please have more?"

"You may." He raised his arm and got to work. Laying one blow after another on his boy's ass, thighs, and shoulders. Nikki hissed and panted, moans low and grateful, and Bradford felt something deep in his soul break away and dissolve as if it were a scab or a bandage, something he suddenly didn't need anymore. His arm felt stronger, freer than it had in a long while. It was astonishing.

He lost track of how many blows he'd dealt, but he was watching Nikki intently, listening, all his senses focused on his sub. He let up on the power but not the speed, letting lighter blows fall on Nikki's hot skin, and listened closely as the boy's moans broke up into a soft hum.

"Good, boy," he said, his tone soothing and low. He wasn't surprised that Nikki didn't reply, he just kept talking as he gradually brought the flogging to an end and tossed the instrument aside. "I am very pleased, my boy."

Nikki was down deep somewhere, perhaps even beyond customary subspace, and Bradford was thrilled. He'd celebrate privately later. For now, his sub most certainly needed him.

He released Nikki's feet first, admiring his work and the deep red skin on Nikki's thighs. From there he kept contact, running his hands over every bit of Nikki that he safely could within the boundaries of their agreement. He removed the cuffs on Nikki's wrists, but Nikki held them in place until he stepped alongside his boy and coaxed them down. "That's my boy. Good boy."

Nikki leaned against him, tucking that blond head into his shoulder and he was mildly surprised to discover that Nikki was hard. And not a little. The boy's cock curved upward stiffly and was nearly as red as the boy's ass.

Well that was rather fascinating, wasn't it? He was half-hard himself, which was no surprise to him at all after a satisfying flogging, but he forced himself to put away the wonderfully filthy things he was imagining, so he could focus on his boy.

His boy, who had not agreed to sexual contact of any kind.

He led Nikki over to the divan and retrieved the lotion he'd used after their last session. The scent was soothing and hopefully familiar enough to Nikki to bring back feelings of comfort. "Kneel, boy. I'd let you sit with me, but your skin is far too sensitive right now.

Nikki knelt, still silent. That was fine, the sub was deep in his space and compliant, he didn't require verbal acknowledgment.

"That's it, boy. Why don't you rest your head in my lap?"

He settled himself and helped Nikki maneuver so his sub could comfortably rest on his knees, and accepted Nikki's weight as the boy leaned heavily into him. For a short while, he did nothing more than run his fingers through the boy's hair, just touching gently, waiting for Nikki to recover a bit. Nikki had started to stir by the time he'd reached for the lotion.

With great care, he applied lotion to the red skin on his boy's back. He couldn't help but trace a line here and a line there with his fingers where the harsher leather falls had raised the skin, and each time he got a lovely moan from his boy.

"How are you feeling?" he asked finally.

"Good, sir." Nikki's voice rough and low. "I feel so good."

Bradford wasn't sure whether to be amused or insulted as Nikki's hand wrapped around that lovely, ruddy erection and started stroking. Nikki moaned, arm pumping. Bradford knew he wasn't going to let the boy continue, but he allowed himself to take it in for a moment. He was Master after all, and he could have what pleased him. But there was a lesson here, one of many along these lines that Nikki had yet to learn, and he could only allow himself to indulge for so long.

"Very pretty, boy. I bet that feels good."

"Yes. Yes...sir. Ah."

He shook his head. God, he remembered being twenty like it was yesterday. "*Enough.*"

"Ah!" Nikki cried out and rocked forward.

"Have I given you permission to get off, boy?"

"...no, sir."

"Have I given you permission to touch yourself? To stroke and pleasure yourself? Well, boy? Have I?"

"No...sir! I'm sorry, sir."

His raised voice would have to be enough for now as they hadn't yet discussed discipline and punishment. He noted that although Nikki was distressed, the boy didn't appear ready to use safe words. "Sit up, boy."

As soon as Nikki was upright again, he stood and paced away. "Forearms on the floor, forehead on your hands, ass the air, knees spread. Now." He kept his tone stern and clipped.

"Yes, sir."

He watched Nikki work through his orders, remaining silent until the boy had settled and was still. "Knees wider. Ass higher."

"Yes, sir." Nikki complied.

He walked a slow circle around the boy, checking his posture, making sure Nikki was in a position he could hold for a while. "Earlier you learned display. This position I call 'supplication.' Pay attention to it, know what it feels like, because the next time you end up here—and I assure you, you will—I won't instruct you. And I'll be less patient than I am right now."

Nikki nodded.

"What was that, boy?"

"Yes, sir. I will remember it, sir," Nikki answered quickly, voice shaking a little. Bradford kept a close eye on the boy but let him worry a little.

"You do nothing without my permission, boy."

"I'm sorry, sir."

"You are to be focusing on pleasing me. Your mind, your actions, and your body are mine to command. If you need something, you may ask for it. If I say no, you may beg if you feel you need to. I may still say no. Was stroking yourself off thinking of me?"

"No, sir," Nikki said sullenly.

"I can't hear you, boy."

"No, sir!"

"No, it was thinking of your own needs. It was putting your needs ahead of mine."

"I'm sorry, sir." To Nikki's credit, the boy did sound truly contrite.

"Are you sure?" Time for the harder questions.

"Sir?"

"Tell me what you did wrong."

"I...yes, sir. I wanted...I was so hard, and I was in this...I was floating, and I just *wanted* and it felt so good. I wasn't focused. I wasn't...you want this, don't you? That's what Cade told me. No one says no to you."

Bradford snorted, one eyebrow climbing toward his hairline. Cade would hear about that one. "What do you take me for, boy? Do not try to manipulate me. Sex—getting off in any manner—is not in our agreement, and it is therefore out of the question. We follow rules and contracts in this lifestyle for a reason."

"I'm sorry, sir."

"Tell me again."

"I'm sorry, sir."

"Again."

"I'm sorry! Sir, please. I was wrong."

"That's better, boy. Tell me more."

"I...I was wrong. I didn't understand. I am still learning." Nikki's shoulders started to tremble, and his fingers curled against the floor. "I want to learn to be better. I want to please you, I do, I promise. I know this is good for me, sir. I've never trusted anyone like this. I've never felt so *real*. Please, sir. I'm sorry."

He nodded. He hated to browbeat the boy, but some lessons were better learned by example. A lesson learned, however, deserved a reward. He sat on the floor next to Nikki's head and stroked the boy's hair. "You are real, boy. It will be my priority as your Master to remain worthy of your trust. You made a mistake, and you're attempting to learn from it. I can't ask anything more of you than that. You have pleased me."

Nikki stayed still as stone, his voice contrite. "It won't happen again, sir."

"Oh, my boy, I can assure you it will. And that's all right. Mistakes are human, and you have so much to learn yet. You will make them, you will learn, and I will forgive. You will have hard days. You will also have whole weeks where everything seems perfect, and then something will throw you. It happens. I expect it, and you should accept that." He would have off days as well, but that wasn't something he was going to say right now. Anticipating his needs that way would be something the boy would learn as they got to know one another better in this context.

"Kneeling display, boy."

Nikki obeyed, taking a moment to arrange himself as Bradford stood.

"Shoulders back. Chin up. Yes, like that." Nikki made the small adjustments easily, and he noted his sub's lovely erection was dissipating and a very pretty, softer cock hung in its place. "Good boy."

They had much to talk about. Nikki was so new on the one hand, and yet in some ways the boy was well ahead of many of the club's more experienced subs. His instincts were lovely, his tolerance—his desire—for the sting of Bradford's flogger, and the boy's still-undiscovered depth was enticing and delicious.

"All right, boy. A new lesson." Bradford walked around behind Nikki so the boy could concentrate on the words and not worry so much about his eyes or his body language. "Conceptually, submission is very simple. At its most basic, you relinquish your own will and you submit to mine. That sounds easy, but in reality, I know it isn't. Especially for someone who is accustomed to being self-reliant, hm? You have gone a very long time—many years—relying on yourself without assistance or support. Not because you wanted to, but because you had to. Am I right?"

"Yes, sir," Nikki replied simply.

"When you spend so much time worrying about the basic needs of your body—food, shelter, safety—you aren't able to spend time on the needs of your soul. But I have seen those needs, boy. You've shown them to me. And I have heard them in your words, when you tell me that you feel *real*, you feel *free*. I believe it has been there all this time, the way you crave being relieved of responsibility, and I want to take it from you and open up a new path. One in which you will serve me and in exchange your every need will be fully met. That is what the next forty or so hours will be about. We will talk when it's over and discuss how it felt to you. And you always have your words."

Bradford paced away a bit, giving Nikki a chance to catch up, to think.

"I expect mistakes, and please don't worry. I will forgive them. I expect your emotions and your sense of self will get in the way sometimes and make it difficult for you. That's normal and understandable. My only requirement is that you do your best to overcome those things. Do your best, and I will not be disappointed. Avoid making the same mistake twice, and I will be quite pleased. Recognize and acknowledge your issues honestly as they come up, and you will make me proud."

He leaned forward and placed his hand on Nikki's spine between the boy's shoulder blades. "Breathe, boy."

He grinned as Nikki took an enormously deep breath.

"I know it's difficult, but trust me when I tell you that you can't disappoint me if I can tell you're trying. I promise."

"I trust you, sir."

That was the truth. He knew he had the boy's trust, and that was remarkable. "Good boy." He lifted his hand away and continued. "There is more to our evening together, but I think we're done in this room. How do you feel?"

"Warm. A little sore. Fine, sir. Good."

He nodded. "Fetch my jacket from the closet, boy, and help me on with it."

Nikki stood and moved to the closet, not rushing, but the boy's movements were economical, purposeful. He slipped his arms into the jacket as the boy held it open for him.

"Good. You will straighten up in here and dress, return our keys to the bar, then come home. I will be in my study. Use the restroom and meet me there."

"Yes, sir."

"And, boy. Make absolutely sure you feel ready to serve me before you open my study door. Take your time, I don't expect you in a hurry."

"Yes, sir. I will, sir."

"Good boy." Bradford cupped Nikki's cheek, smiling. The boy's eyes were low, but Bradford felt him lean in. "Lovely, boy." He turned and left the room.

17

The party hadn't even started, and it had already been a busy day. Nikki knelt close by while Bradford—while *Sir* got a manicure, a facial, and a straight-razor shave from this barber who actually came to the brownstone. The guy had hot washcloths and the weird shaving cream in a cup and a strap, or *strop*, or whatever it was called. Nikki spent a bunch of time helping Sir dress in a seriously sweet tux tailored to Sir and made of black silk with a soft leather collar, and a pair of shoes that Nikki had polished over and over until they sparkled.

Nikki also helped Sir fasten on a pair of black onyx and platinum cufflinks with the letter "H" on them, that Sir said he wore every amam on his birthday, though he hadn't said why.

Sir was in a great mood, looked amazing in all black, and seemed totally ready for a party.

Nikki was ready too—well, dressed anyway. He was still working on his headspace and trying to get over his nerves. He was standing in display in the middle of Sir's bedroom, wearing all white, which was the dress code for the party:

subs in white, Doms in black. Sir put him in a toga-style wrap of all things that...well, apart from a sort of nod to modesty, wasn't really much of anything. That was part of what made him nervous, though he knew there would be boys wearing even less.

He missed his leather harness a little. It was strange how it had become a bit of a security blanket, reminding him where he was and telling everyone he belonged there. It helped him remember to stand up straight too. It was funny though—every time Sir walked by, Nikki's shoulders would pull back a little. He found himself wanting to please Sir more and more.

God, Nikki. Focus. Why was this so hard?

He closed his eyes for a second, mentally shaking his head at himself. He took a deep breath, let it out slowly, and tried to concentrate.

"Excellent, my boy."

He smiled. Sir didn't miss anything. "Thank you, sir."

In the two weeks since he'd made that horrible mistake in their scene together, Sir had been working with him and talking through the basics, in-scene and out. Sometimes as a sub under an agreement for the evening or a day, but sometimes just in the kitchen over breakfast. They'd talked about ways that he could practice letting his own needs go when he was serving and try to anticipate Sir's needs instead.

He was enjoying this. The trust. The learning, the mistakes and the joy of knowing he'd be forgiven. He still didn't understand why he was drawn to the cross and the sting of Sir's instruments, but he was. And that place he went inside his head was...it felt like safety. It felt like freedom. It made him feel kind of...high almost. Sir told him understanding would come, that it took time, but they would find it together.

Somehow that was okay. Nikki believed him.

It was amazing. Despite being given so much, Sir never asked him to be anyone else. When he wasn't serving, he still came and went when he wanted to, had days off to himself, and he still did his job with Levi as his boss. Sir told him all the time that living this lifestyle was his choice; he was free to come and go as he pleased, that his restrictions were only valid when they were under an agreement—

Whoa. Time to reel it in. He pictured a red dot in the center of his forehead and mentally stared at it, practicing the mantra he'd taught himself to keep his mind from wandering.

How can I best serve Sir—right now?

The answer was easy. Right now, Sir wanted him to be still, and think about the rules for tonight. He ran them through in his head. Meet no one's eyes, even other subs. Stay close to Sir's shoulder but don't hide back there. Speak only when directly spoken to. Expect to do a lot of kneeling. Stay focused—obviously the hardest rule of all for him tonight.

He wasn't nervous about the rules. He wasn't even all that nervous about making a mistake. What made him nervous, what that now very familiar part of him was actually dreading, were all the eyes that would be on him. The Doms and the subs looking at him and knowing that Sir had chosen him tonight. That of all the subs at the club, most of whom had much more experience than he did, Sir had chosen him for this party. It felt like a lot of pressure.

Sir had proposed a compromise, where he and Brian would alternate serving, so that Nikki could go somewhere private and breathe every once in a while if the social thing got too heavy. Sir said Brian had agreed easily, and no wonder. Brian was always eager to serve Sir. And it was good to know that he could have a little freak-out if he needed to.

"Are you ready, boy?"

No?

"Yes, sir." Nikki leaned into Sir's hand where it cupped his cheek.

"My boy. What am I asking of you tonight?"

"That I do my best, sir."

"Just so, boy. I can't ask more of you than that."

You say that all the time.

"Naturally, there will be near-perfect subs in attendance with years of training. I don't need perfection. You will see subs that can walk to heel without falter. I don't need that from you, either. Perfection, a beautiful showing, is admirable to be sure. But a boy who is earnest and wants to please can be even more impressive. The members will see how sincere you are in your desire to serve me and will forgive any fault."

Bradford sounded so sure, and really, he owned the club. He should know.

"I want to make you proud, sir."

Sir leaned in and kissed him on the cheek, the affection reassuring and thrilling at the same time. "That was an excellent beginning. Shall we?"

He smiled and followed Bradford toward the doors to the club, the private ones leading from the brownstone. Allowing kisses had been his idea. He still wasn't ready to add sex into things, but he'd gifted Sir an agreement for his birthday that included kissing. Sir had been pleased and appreciative.

"Breathe, boy. Eyes down, no more than an arm's length

from my shoulder. Speak only if spoken to, or if you need something. Remember your Master believes in you."

"Yes, sir. Thank you, sir." He took a deep breath and followed Sir through the doors and into the dining room.

They were fashionably late, of course, and the dining room was busy. Sir was a bit of a showman, and Nikki knew the man liked to make an entrance. Nearly every table was in use, and the large round table in the center of the room was a sea of black and white, full of Sir's personally invited guests, subs kneeling next to their chairs. As they approached that table, Sir pointed to the floor and he knelt as smoothly as he could manage, settling into his display position. He kept his eyes on the floor, but he could feel Sir's friends looking at him, heard his name.

"Happy Birthday, old man!"

"Stunning, Bradford. Nikki looks great. I'm a fan of the toga."

"Goodness, you old pervert, your boy is young. How long have you been working with him?"

Breathe. Breathe. You belong to Sir, he has your back. Breathe. How can you best serve him—right now?

He checked his posture, relaxing into it, willing the physical act to outweigh his mental struggle.

"We've been working together in earnest for a month or so now. Perhaps a little longer. And he is twenty, but his youth hasn't been anything but an asset so far."

"I'll bet," someone said, and the table laughed.

"Ah, Kent. I must ask you not to embarrass the boy, he's working very hard tonight."

There was a short pause and then a voice, Master Kent's he guessed, said, "Of course. My apologies, Bradford."

"Thank you."

"He looks wonderful, and so eager. That's a gift you're giving your Master, boy. A lovely gift."

Oh, God. Someone is talking to me. Do I say 'Yes, sir'? 'Thank you'? Something else? He tried not to panic.

A hand settled on his back. "You may thank Master Arturo, boy."

Oh, thank God. An answer. He nodded. "Yes, sir." That came out kind of strangled, so he cleared his throat and tried again. "Thank you, Master Arturo."

"You are most welcome. Not to worry, boy. Everyone was new once. The other boys around this table all remember what it was like when they were starting out."

"Good boy." Sir whispered to him, squeezed his shoulder, and went back to the guests.

He took a deep breath and checked his posture again, willing his fingers to stop shaking. He was okay, right? Sir totally got it and was right there. He was okay. *You're okay.*

Sir chatted with the men at the table for a while longer, and Nikki was relieved to feel the focus shift away from him and onto regular things like dinner, wine, golf games, music, and sports scores. He let himself float a little, paying attention to his shoulders, his hands, his spine, his breathing, the feel of the fabric of his toga against his bare skin.

He checked his concentration, but he knew he didn't need to. He was doing this right. How could he best serve Sir right now?

He was already doing it.

A little thrill ran through him, knowing he was doing his best, happy to be pleasing Sir. He only savored it for a moment though, not wanting to get distracted now that he'd finally found the zone.

"Come, boy." Bradford's voice cut through his tight

concentration. When he stood to follow, he noticed that most of the men were already well into their meals, but... just a moment ago they hadn't yet been served, right? When had they gotten their food? He blinked, wondering at the lost time, but he didn't linger on it. His thoughts belonged to his Master.

"Yes, sir." He stepped in behind Bradford's shoulder. His eyes were low and his mind on his responsibilities, but he heard Brian whisper as the other boy stepped in alongside him.

"You look great."

He wasn't sure if speaking only when spoken to applied to other subs, so he didn't reply, he just nodded his head at Brian. Brian reached over and squeezed his fingers.

18

"This was a wonderful party as always, Bradford." Reed shook Bradford's hand, his broad smile genuine.

"Did you enjoy your dinner?"

"I did. My salmon was just wonderful. I enjoyed the jazz band, the dancing, the cocktails...the whole thing reminded me very much of one of Harrison's parties from the old days. I imagine that was deliberate, hm?"

He smiled. It had been, though all these years later, Bradford continued to keep his relationship with the club's venerated former owner to himself. It was hard to believe, however, that Reed had no idea. It was even possible Harrison had told Reed, as they had been close friends. "I may have been feeling nostalgic."

Reed gave his shoulder a squeeze. "Everyone that knew him misses his presence. But I can say with certainty that he would be very proud of the way you've made the club your own and still honored his tradition in the process. I know I am."

As a member of what he thought of as the old guard of the club, the compliment was especially meaningful to him.

"Thank you, sir." He took a breath and looked at the sub behind Reed's shoulder. "Did you enjoy your evening, Noah?"

"I did, sir. Thank you. It was a lovely party." The boy smiled. "Master Reed is an accomplished dance partner."

He chuckled. Reed had at one time been a ballroom dance instructor. "I should hope so. How are the two of you getting on?"

"Ah. Not as Noah had hoped, I'm afraid. I asked the boy to serve me for your party, but we likely won't be working together long-term, unfortunately. I have great respect for Noah's skill, however. He has been well trained."

Dammit. Why not? "I'm sorry to hear that."

"I'm negotiating with another sub for the long-term. He was unable to be here this evening."

"A member?" Bradford raised an eyebrow.

"Not yet. I'll call you in a couple of days if things work out as I hope they will."

"Please do." He looked at Noah again. "Well. I'm sorry, boy. Let's talk again this week at your convenience."

"Yes, sir. I'll call you." Noah nodded to him, eyes still respectfully low.

"I've just promised to call the boy a car home, Bradford. If you'll excuse us."

"Yes, of course. Good night, gentlemen."

How was it possible he couldn't find a long-term match for one of the most skilled and respected subs at the club? Well. He'd work with Noah himself short-term if need be. He felt terrible for testing the match now, but he couldn't have known about Reed's potential arrangement with a sub outside of the club.

He looked down at Nikki, who had knelt beside him

while he and Reed were talking, and ruffled his boy's hair. "Come along, boy."

Nikki managed to stay by his side for most of the party, and Bradford was very pleased about that. Brian only spelled the boy twice, and the rest of the evening he was able to show off two lovely, young subs at heel. Not a bad birthday present at all.

The black and white theme had been quite popular, with Doms and subs alike enjoying the look, and the very obvious indication of status. Some couples followed the color rule with black and white leather, some went for more stylized or upscale looks with outfits that hinted at tuxedos. A handful of couples went full-on costume party and were things like a devil and an angel, Batman and a nurse, and even Danny and Sandy from Grease.

So much fun.

Nikki and Brian's matching short, white togas had been a hit, and Bradford had gone with his favorite black silk suit and Harrison's cufflinks, which had essentially become his birthday party uniform at this point.

He wasn't a young man anymore, so now that his party was at a low simmer and the evening had started to wear on, he whisked Nikki off to a room for a very short scene before turning in. Only a nightcap really, nothing heavy or lengthy, just something to make sure they were connecting and to reward his boy for a truly perfect evening. Thankfully, he'd arranged for Brian, Joe, Liam, and Andrew to close up the club after the party, so he could escort Nikki home and turn in whenever he pleased.

He looked at the boy, kneeling in front of him, chin high and eyes low, and marveled at how far Nikki had come. At how happy the boy seemed. There was really only one reward—well, one the boy would allow—for all this. He'd put the boy on the cross. He'd take the kisses that were offered to him while he could, then he'd give himself an orgasm to cap off the evening.

"Boy."

"Sir?" Nikki was deeply settled and had been working hard to stay that way. He couldn't have been more proud or more pleased by how the evening had gone.

"You've been such a good boy tonight, I'm very proud of you."

"Thank you, sir. Are you enjoying your birthday?"

Such a sweetheart. "I am, I have. I want to offer you a reward for all of your hard work."

"Knowing that you're proud of me is a reward, sir."

"Oh, my boy. Knowing I am proud of you is rewarding, but not a reward. It should make you feel proud too. A reward is something for you, something you've earned for making me proud."

"Thank you, sir."

"Stand up, boy."

"Yes, sir." Nikki stood, so petite even at full height. Just lovely.

"I'm allowed kisses tonight per our contract, am I not?"

"Yes, sir. For your birthday."

"Birthday kisses. Such a sweet and thoughtful gift." He smiled. He hated to think what would happen if their next contract disallowed them again, but for now he was going to take full advantage. He cupped Nikki's jaw, fingers sliding along the bone, and tilted the boy's face to his. The way Nikki's lips parted for him was pure perfection and he took the offer, pressing their lips together.

He thought he might have been satisfied with just that much, but Nikki offered more, opening for him and inviting his tongue, gentle hands reaching out to rest on his chest.

He hadn't intended to moan, or to pull the boy in so close, but Nikki didn't resist; the boy just melted into his arms.

Oh, God. He'd known it would be sweet, but he never thought kissing Nikki would make him feel...this. It was as if he hadn't felt anything at all in such a long, long time. Suddenly pieces of him were bright and clear again, pieces that he hadn't shelved away exactly, but he hadn't acknowledged in years, either.

He broke the kiss and looked into those bright blue eyes. All he wanted was more. Nikki whimpered and went up on his toes, asking for more as well, but he knew better. They had an agreement.

"To the cross, boy," he made himself say, not surprised by the rough hint of need in his voice. This was meant to be Nikki's reward, not a self-indulgent fantasy about the things he hadn't been offered and couldn't be sure he ever would.

Nikki had already slipped out of his toga and was wearing nothing but a pair of tight shorts. The bright white of the fabric made the boy's pale skin seem more like smooth cream. He took a breath and removed his shirt so he could move better, carefully setting the cufflinks aside before going to the wall to select a flogger. The one he chose was heavier than the last one he'd used with Nikki; the tips would probably raise a few welts, leave marks that he would have to tend to, but aftercare was part of the process and good for them both.

He stuck the flogger in his belt and knelt to fasten Nikki's feet into the cross. "Give me your words, boy."

"Nickel and dime, sir."

" 'Nickel and dime,' good boy. I've chosen an intermediate flogger. I'll go easy, but remember to use your words if you need them. Your honesty pleases me—it's not about how much you can take but about making sure I understand your needs. Setting limits is important. Use them if you need them."

"Yes, sir."

He took note of the hungry bulge in Nikki's shorts and was glad he let the boy keep them on. He only had so much self-control.

Bradford stood and strapped Nikki's wrists in, listening to the deep breaths his boy was taking and the comfort Nikki took in just the bondage alone. When he was done, he let his hands move over Nikki's skin, tracing the slope of his boy's shoulders and the line down to Nikki's narrow waist.

He followed that by placing a light kiss between Nikki's shoulder blades and smiled as his boy drew in a sighing breath. "Sir."

It was possible that sort of kiss wasn't strictly contracted, so he waited to see if Nikki would protest, but heard nothing.

He swung the flogger through the air, testing the weight and balance. He knew this one well and didn't need much practice, but he wanted Nikki to hear it and anticipate.

"All right boy, we'll get started."

"Yes, sir. I'm ready."

"Remember to breathe."

He raised his arm twice, bringing the flogger down high on each of Nikki's shoulders. The sound was loud and satisfying and Nikki cried out, rocking against the cross. "Oh, God."

Bradford paused, watching his boy's beautiful pale skin turn pink and giving Nikki a moment to recover. "I don't hear words, boy."

"No, sir. I..." Nikki took a deep breath and let it out, his stance still strong. "I'm ready."

Nikki's reward was going to be a gift to them both. "Good

---

boy. Two more then, just a hair lower." He didn't hesitate and landed two more blows, exactly where he'd intended.

The boy moaned softly and nodded. "Thank you, sir."

He hadn't requested thanks, and the beauty of the offer left him a bit winded. He took a step away, making sure his focus was where it should be before swinging the flogger in the air once more and returning to his spot behind his boy. "You are welcome. A few more now, remember your words and call them out loud if you need to."

"Yes, sir. So ready."

Bradford let his arm fly, counting six, seven, eight satisfying blows without a safe word before he stopped and went to Nikki to make sure his boy was well and whole.

Nikki was moaning softly and sweating lightly, but he seemed steady on his feet. "How do you feel, boy?"

"Good," the boy answered immediately. Nikki's voice was rough but not weak, and his expression was beautiful and blissed out. "So good. Oh, God."

All the same, he stalled a bit by inspecting the welts and stroking Nikki's shoulders and arms with soothing fingers. "Such a good boy," he whispered. "Beautiful."

Nikki arched toward him, the boy's ass pressing into his groin. "Oh, sir. You're hard." The boy did it again, this time grinding into him much more deliberately.

He lost himself in the friction, groaning and wanting. "Boy."

"Your boy."

"Oh, Nikki." He tucked the flogger into his belt and dug his fingers into Nikki's hips, letting the boy tease and feeling his own desire begin to settle into his balls.

"Touch me. Please, sir. Please?"

He moaned and reached for Nikki, fingers just grazing

the boy's erection before he snatched his hand back and stepped away.

"Sir?"

Dammit, he was hard as granite, and he wasn't thinking clearly. He took a deep breath, steeling himself against his own hunger, and watched Nikki closely. *Not part of our agreement*, he reminded himself sternly. Nikki was floating and vulnerable, and as much as he wanted the boy, he knew better.

"Sir! Please."

"That's not in our contract, boy."

"It's okay. I want you, I do. Please."

"No, boy. I won't. That would break my promise to you. It would violate our agreement." His voice was rough as gravel, and he had to work to be sure he was heard.

Nikki whimpered and started slowly humping the cross, and he watched, mesmerized as that pretty ass clenched and rolled, and listened to Nikki's breath hitch.

"Enough, boy," he said finally, but Nikki didn't seem to hear. He cleared his throat and tried again. "That's *enough*, boy!"

Nikki froze, panting, everything in the boy's body going still and tense.

"You do not have my permission to—"

"Dime, sir!"

Hearing that safe word was shocking, and Bradford went immediately into safety mode. He tossed his flogger to the floor and stepped close to Nikki, reaching for the boy's cuffs. "I'm right here, boy. Let me get you down. Have I injured you?"

"No, sir."

He couldn't imagine he had, but he had to ask anyway. He took a deep breath and quickly freed Nikki's feet first and then the boy's hands trying to let go of his initial panic at hearing the boy's hard-stop safe word. "What is it, boy? What happened?"

Nikki stepped into him and pulled him down for a kiss. He blinked and broke it off almost immediately, pushing the boy out to arm's length. "Nikki?"

"I ended the scene. That ends our agreement, right?"

What? Did he...was he hearing that right? "What?"

"I ended the contract with my safe word. That means we can fuck now, right?"

"Nikki—"

"You want to, I know you do."

"No." He shoved Nikki back a step and Nikki blinked at him, looking wounded.

"N...no?"

Jesus Christ. "Well, yes. But not now. Not—" He shook his head. "Kneel, boy."

"Bradfo—"

"*Goddamnit.* I said kneel, boy."

At Bradford's shout, Nikki gasped and dropped to his knees like he'd been hamstrung, gaze falling to the floor. "Sir—"

"Not another word." He took a deep breath, trying to get his temper under control. His temper, his goddamn libido... what in the name of God was happening here?

Nikki went silent and still, and that made it easier to think. To concentrate. He rolled the last few minutes over in his mind, trying to figure out where he'd gone wrong. Where Nikki had made a mistake. Where their evening went off the rails and became...this.

On the one hand, it was simple to distill this down into something coherent; he was a pervy old man with a hard-on, and Nikki was lovely and sweet and wanted him. Be that as it may, that wasn't everything. That wasn't a fair representation of what had happened here.

They'd kissed. Bradford certainly hadn't expected that moment to be as powerful as it was, and he presumed the boy hadn't, either. He'd thought it would be all in good fun. A little tease and nothing more. He wasn't sure which of them had led them down a different path, but it was most certainly his responsibility. There was no question he wanted Nikki, and until tonight he'd been very in control of that hunger...right up until they'd kissed, and Nikki offered him a much deeper, more intimate connection than he had been prepared for.

Had this been someone like Noah, a sub with great experience, Bradford would be handling this differently. An experienced sub like Noah would have been well aware of what they were doing, and Bradford would likely have dealt out a harsh punishment for attempting to break their contract. But Nikki was green, and Bradford was obligated to be teacher and mentor first, Dom second. And lover was... well, at this point it was far behind all that. Allowing behavior strictly forbidden by their contract would be irresponsible at best, and an outright violation of trust at its worst. What would the boy learn from that?

He paced away a few steps, thinking, forming his thoughts into words.

"Contracts are carefully and respectfully negotiated, and then followed to the letter. Heat of the moment decisions in-scene are not safe or sane, and in a case like this one, in which you—

in which the *sub*—is floating on endorphins, to diverge so drastically from a contract's provisions could not reasonably be considered consensual."

He said it out loud both to hear it himself and to give

Nikki something to think about. He paced the room, moving past Nikki without pause.

"I refused your advances because it is my duty to see that your needs as you have expressed them to me, are met, and your boundaries respected. You put that trust in me when we made our agreement."

"But—"

"Nikki!"

Dammit!

Temper, Bradford. Control your emotions. You do not maintain a man's respect by shouting.

Harrison's words filled his mind as if the man were standing right next to him, both startling and soothing him at once.

Save me from myself, Harry. I want this boy like I haven't wanted anyone since I had you.

He needed to breathe, get perspective, sort this out for himself. And although he desperately wanted to, he knew he couldn't just send Nikki away. The boy's skin needed tending to at the very least. He walked over to Nikki and rested a hand against the boy's cheek. Nikki silently leaned into the touch, understandably seeking reassurance. They stayed like that until Bradford felt them both breathing easier, then ordered Nikki to the couch along the far wall.

"Lie on your stomach and I will tend to your back, boy."

Nikki moved silently to the couch, head down, eyes low. He knew the boy had to be contending with need, arousal, and a host of conflicting emotions: everything from rejection to embarrassment. He felt for the boy; this was a tough lesson and Nikki was going to have to sit with it for a while.

He went to the first aid kit and pulled out ointment and an ice pack and got to work.

19

After that disaster, Sir—Bradford—led Nikki to the brownstone, brought him Tylenol and tea, and tucked him into bed.

Like he mattered, like he was worth all that fuss.

But Nikki didn't feel worth it at all.

He did sleep some, but he woke up in the darkness of the middle of the night and couldn't go back to sleep. His heart hurt. His mind was racing. He couldn't be at Bradford's right now. Everything he looked at reminded him where he was, who owned the place.

He couldn't think.

Nikki got out of bed, pulled on jeans and a hoodie, then headed out into the late-night-quiet street. Despite the light rain, it was a decent night for a walk. But even if it hadn't been, he was pretty sure he'd be out walking in it anyway.

He didn't need to think too hard about where to go at least. His feet took him downtown toward the paved paths along the river, and the public park where he'd spent most of his nights before he met Bradford. Before he got his first ever job.

Well, not his first job, but his first legit job.

The longer he walked through the familiar streets, the more his mind wandered. He kept getting distracted. His night with Bradford came back to him as sounds and images in his mind. The smell of the leather-covered cross in the playroom. The sweet sting of Bradford's flogger. The velvet warmth of Bradford's tongue gliding along his own. The undeniable ache of his hard-on.

The edge in Bradford's voice.

Jesus, he'd fucked up good this time. And on Bradford's birthday of all days, when all he'd wanted to do was—

All he'd wanted to do was please his Dom. Make Bradford happy. Offer his Master a gift.

Instead he'd lost his shit and broken some sacred rule of contracts or fucking or something he didn't understand. He'd insulted the man. He'd made Bradford angry.

God, he was so fucking embarrassed. Humiliated. He ought to have known. By now he should have understood the rules. He should have known better than to think he could belong in that world.

He should have known he'd fuck something up eventually.

He looked great in leather, in his harness, rubbing elbows with men that had money and were way smarter than he was. But the harness was just his ticket into the club. Nikki would never have what those men had, never be what those other subs were, no matter what Bradford said.

No matter how hard he tried.

He took a deep breath and tried to let it go. Dark night, wet street...this felt better, being out here in the damp quiet. This was familiar.

He walked beside the dark water along a path that was well lit in some places and hardly at all in others. He used to sleep in those shadows. He could go all night unnoticed by people walking in the light. Maybe he'd sleep out here tonight, find one of his old spots where he could think about what to do next. Where to go.

He walked a long while, until the rain started coming down harder and he'd run out of path. His friends—his former friends—the ones that turned tricks, knew this area of the park better than he did. But he knew if he followed the dark path around, it came out on the street where Kit lived in this apartment with a bunch of other guys. It was a pit, but it was out of the rain, and they'd let him crash there tonight.

"Take a walk?" A voice behind him asked, startling him into turning around. "Twenty bucks."

Fuck. "I'm not—sorry. I don't do that."

"Twenty bucks to suck my cock."

"Not happening." Nikki started walking away, staying in the light.

The guy followed him and crowded him against a low wall. "Come on you little prick. I'll give you thirty."

"No. Not twenty, not thirty. Not happening. Fuck off." *Don't look scared.*

This wasn't Nikki's first experience out here, but this guy wasn't taking no for an answer.

"Why are you out here then, pretty boy?" The guy's hand landed in his groin. Nikki made a fist and took the first punch, heart pounding. A kid had taught him a lesson his second night on the street, and the words played over, loudly, in his head.

If you're going to try to take him down, you better make sure he can't get back up.

So Nikki threw a second punch, then grabbed the guy by the shoulders and planted a knee in his crotch. The guy cried out and doubled over, and Nikki took off running.

But he didn't get far.

———

"I'm really glad you called me." Brian was standing in front of Nikki, hands in his pockets.

"Fucking cops." Nikki lifted the ice pack off his knuckles and looked at his hand, wincing at the bruising and the split skin. He'd had to call someone, and he'd thought hard about who it should be. Then he'd remembered Brian helping Levi home from the bar, how discreet the guy had been about that, and kind too. He'd decided Brian was the one to call.

"Weren't you scared? That guy might have come after you, Nikki. At least now he's in custody."

"Have you ever tried to explain fresh stripes from a flogger to a guy in a cop uniform? They assumed I was a whore, Brian. They thought I was—I mean do you know what that feels like?"

"I...no." Brian looked down at his shoes.

Nikki looked at his friend and sighed. "I'm sorry, Brian. I'm just...really tired. Just ignore me. I appreciate you coming out here to get me." Fuck, his hand hurt. The EMTs had a look and said it wasn't broken, so he'd refused treatment at the hospital, but he was starting to have second thoughts about that now. He maybe could have asked for something to help him sleep. "Can you get me out of here, please?"

Brian looked at him and shook his head. "I can't. I was told you have to wait for paperwork."

Nikki stood up with a growl, the frustration of his whole

evening starting to bubble over. "God *dammit*!"

"Hey." Brian stood up and followed him, put a hand on his chest. "It's okay, Nikki. Just breathe. We'll go home and talk, okay? I'll make some cocoa or tea or something. I'm a good listener, I swear. Just stay calm so we can get out of here."

Calm? He wasn't sure he had any calm in him tonight. Not anymore. But Brian was cool to come get him, and he didn't want to get in more trouble. Thank God he was over eighteen, they used to hold him and try to call his parents.

"Mr. Richards?"

"Oh! Over here, sir." Brian called out.

Nikki turned around, holding the ice on his aching knuckles. "Can I go home, please?"

"This is a copy of your paperwork. If we need to contact you, we'll use the number you put down there. Take care of that hand and have a good night."

Brian took all the paperwork for him. "Thank you, officer. You too."

Nikki really hoped they wouldn't need to contact him. He just wanted to forget tonight even happened. All of it. Everything.

Brian put an arm around his waist and led him outside into the rain. It was pouring now. "God, what an awful night for all of this."

"I don't think there's such a thing as a good one."

Brian pulled him under an awning and brushed his wet bangs out of his eyes "I guess not."

"I'm fucking humiliated, Brian. And I...I had a bad night."

"I wasn't sure whether or not I should ask. I thought I'd at least find us a cab first. Everything looked great at the party. What happened?"

"Bradford is pissed off at me. I blew it."

"No way. Master Bradford's not mad at you. He doesn't really get mad."

"Well, he was pissed this time. He snapped at me. Shouted." He sighed. "I guess I deserved it, but still."

Brian looked at him, wide-eyed. "Master Bradford? Shouted? I just don't see—"

"I wanted him." They were shouting at each other over the heavy rain hitting the awning over their heads, but it was better than standing out in it. "I wanted him to fuck me, Brian, but it wasn't in our agreement. I didn't realize and then I used my safe word and ended the scene so we could —but I guess that's not how it works, either. I really fucked up. I just wanted—" He'd wanted Bradford. He was floating, high as a kite, but he knew what he wanted. He still knew even now.

"Oh, Nikki." Brian put an arm around his shoulders. "That's why you didn't call Master Bradford? That's why you called me instead?"

"I left. I had to get out of there. I can't go back."

Brian didn't say anything about that, thankfully. He just did what a good friend would do. "You can stay with me."

Nikki nodded, grateful. "Thanks, Brian. I really appreciate that."

"But Nikki, I think maybe it's just a misunderstanding. Master Bradford cares about you. I think you should talk to him"

"Not tonight." He needed to think.

"That's fine. I understand." Brian left him there and went to flag down a cab, and by the time one pulled up, the poor guy was soaked. Brian didn't complain at all, just held the door for him and climbed in after.

"You're a mess, Brian. I'm sorry."

"I'm not a mess. I'm just wet. Are you okay?" Brian took his hand and held the ice on it for him. The guy was so sweet. Just genuinely kind. He hadn't met very many people like that.

"I'm...getting to okay."

"Nikki, I promise you, a bad scene isn't a reason to give up on Master Bradford. He's been doing this a long time. He's seen everything. He's always been so good to me."

He sighed. "We'll see. I have to work on Tuesday."

"So you'll come back to work?"

"Unless he fires me. I need the job." Especially if he was going to have to find a place of his own.

The cab ride didn't take long, and soon he was sitting on Brian's couch in borrowed sweats, his hand wrapped in gauze and drinking a cup of hot cocoa. "Thanks again, Brian."

"I'm really glad you called me. I'm glad you trust me." Brian laid a pillow and a couple of blankets on the couch next to him.

"We're friends."

Brian smiled at him. "I think so, but sometimes it's hard to really know with other subs."

"We're friends," Nikki said again to make his point. "And I appreciate that you went out of your way at a stupid hour in the rain to help me."

Brian sat and put an arm around him. "I'm glad you're okay. That was kind of a scary phone call to get."

It had been a scary night. From the first moment he realized he'd done something wrong to when Brian finally showed up. The whole night had been bad choices, one after another. Bradford would never forgive him.

Never.

20

"Goddamnit, boy." Bradford paced the length of his library, long strides covering ground so quickly that he gave up on back and forth and made it a loop. Past the sofa, around the armchair along the long wall that housed Harrison's book collection, past the antique desk he'd brought in last year, and along the short wall with the tall windows that looked out onto a gray morning.

Apart from being frantic about his boy—the boy, not his boy, *the* boy—he was wrestling with a bubbling cauldron of other unpleasant emotions this morning, and the mix was so potent he couldn't manage to separate them all. Frustration. Exasperation. Melancholy.

Loneliness.

"Dammit."

Had he made a mistake? Should he have made a different decision in the moment?

There was a knock at the door, and he looked up, only then realizing that he'd stopped pacing and was staring out the window at the damp street.

"Come in." He knew it would be Levi; the boy was the

only one he'd confided in thus far about Nikki, and the only one he'd called this morning. "Tell me you have news."

"Yes, sir." Levi walked right to him and knelt at his feet. "Nikki stayed the night at Brian's apartment, he's there now. Brian says he is sleeping and otherwise fine."

"Did you ask Brian to bring him to me?"

"I did, but Brian says that Nikki specifically asked him not to tell you where he is and that he doesn't want to return to the brownstone."

"I see." That wasn't so surprising. But it was goddamn disappointing.

"Is there anything else I can do, sir?" Levi was a good boy. So loyal.

"No, I'm afraid there likely isn't. But I do appreciate your offer, boy. If I think of anything. I will send for you. In the meantime, this remains between us. All right?"

He didn't need a hundred questions or looks from other subs.

"Of course, sir." The boy tried not to sound disappointed, but he knew Levi wanted to stay. Perhaps later. He needed to think about this for a while.

He touched Levi's cheek. "Thank you, boy. You may go. Do let me know if you hear anything more."

"Yes, sir. I will." Levi stood and marched himself back out of the library.

Bradford looked out the window again, wondering what would happen if he picked up his phone and called Brian himself. Would Nikki really refuse to speak to him?

He sighed. That was the prevailing issue, he knew. Doubt. Had he done the right thing by refusing Nikki? Was he too old-fashioned? Were his expectations too high? Was he just a stupid old fool?

He was rarely in doubt. It was the most...uncomfortable feeling to be second-guessing himself.

Uncomfortable to say the least. It was...perturbing. It was bordering on torment.

So there, Harry. I'm a walking thesaurus now.

Harrison would have had the answer of course; his lover always had. It was entirely possible, of course, that Harrison's answer would have been to chastise him for allowing himself to become so smitten with such a lovely young sub in the first place.

But I wouldn't want Nikki the way I do if I still had you, my love.

"I know, Dear Heart."

Bradford sighed and let his eyes close.

————

"You can't just give up, Harry."

The hospital room where Harrison had been for the last month was decorated with cards and flowers sent by members of the club and gifts from the care packages the subs put together every week. They were surrounded by so much support, so many friends. Why wasn't it enough?

It ought to have been enough.

"Yes, I can, love." Harrison licked his lips, and Bradford reached for the water. "I can make that decision, and I have."

Bradford filled a cup and put a straw in it, then held the straw to his lover's lips. Harrison looked so small now, so much older than his years, so much weaker than Bradford would ever have ever thought possible. Harrison had always been a lion to him.

"But I need you."

Harrison's dry laugh stung. "Oh, no, my own. You don't.

You've been running the club on your own, it's yours already. You'll be—"

"I wasn't talking about the club." Damn the club, he'd trade it in a heartbeat for his husband.

Harrison took his hand. "I know. I need you too. I need you to accept that this is my decision and that it doesn't mean I don't love you."

"Harry—"

Harrison reached out and took his hand, fingers bony and cold. "I can't anymore, love. Please, I need you to understand. I've had enough. I want to enjoy the time I have left. I want to spend it with you. At home."

He searched Harrison's eyes and sighed. "I understand."

That was the only lie he'd ever told Harrison, but it was what his husband needed to hear just then, and he was wise enough to understand that. It would be true soon; he'd come to terms with what his husband was asking of him. He'd make sure it wasn't a lie for long.

They brought Harrison home the next afternoon and put him on a tiny dose of morphine that eased his pain and calmed his labored breathing. Harrison never got out of bed again, but they had a few more weeks together. Good weeks, full of talking and reading. Movies. Music.

Until that certain rainy, chilly Thursday evening when Harrison declined to play cards and took his hand again.

"Bradford. I'm tired, Dear Heart. I'm going to sleep now."

Bradford had spent enough time talking with Harrison, listening to his husband, that he finally understood. The treatments in the hospital might have given them some short-term hope, but long-term they were killing Harrison's soul. Here in the brownstone, Harrison had love and friends, good food and his own bed, and he'd been comfortable and happy the last few weeks.

Bradford had known the moment would come, and he'd known it would be too soon. He wasn't ready, but that was as it should be. No one should feel ready to let someone they love go forever. But he had finally accepted that it had to be. He could welcome peace for his husband.

"It's all right, Harry. You can sleep. I love you." He kissed Harrison's lips as his husband closed those beautiful hazel eyes for good.

————

Bradford took two slow steps toward his favorite chair and sat in it heavily. He tried to imagine who he'd be if Harrison hadn't pulled him off the street years ago, but there was no way of knowing. He liked to believe he'd have a roof over his head at least, be responsible and working somewhere, surrounding himself with like-minded people. But he wouldn't have the club, the higher understanding of what and who he was and still could be, the privilege...and he wouldn't have had a husband who believed in him.

Of all those things he knew he'd be missing, having someone who believed in him was the most important thing of all. That realization made the answer to what he needed to do very clear.

He believed in Nikki.

The boy was young and rash and impulsive—all the things that defined being twenty—but also beautiful and smart and a natural sub.

He had no intention of giving up on the boy or punishing him for an honest mistake. But more to the point, he wasn't going to let Nikki give up on himself.

He went to the antique desk, picked up the phone and dialed Levi.

"Hello, sir. Is everything all right?"

"Yes, yes. Fine, Levi, thank you."

"What can I do for you, sir?" Levi sounded so eager.

"Get Brian on the phone, please."

"Yes, sir."

Bradford stood up, intending to pour himself a drink, but remembered the time and went back to his chair. Just his luck he'd have a crisis that required bourbon before noon.

Bradford sat, and waited.

And waited.

When the phone finally rang, he was about ready to tell Levi never mind, but it was Nikki on the line.

"Hello, Bradford."

He held the phone away from his face and sighed so Nikki wouldn't hear. *Bradford*, he noted, not *Sir*.

"Good afternoon. Are you all right?"

"I'm fine. I am."

Of all the things Nikki could have said to him, those were the most important, and Nikki had to know that, because there wasn't a hint of sarcasm. "Thank you, boy. I'm very relieved to hear that."

"I'm...I..." Nikki's sigh seemed almost painful.

Poor boy. "I was relieved to hear that Brian has been looking after you."

"I don't need looking after," Nikki snapped.

"No. No, I'm sorry. That's not precisely what I—"

"I can take care of myself, you know. I did for a long time."

Yes, he remembered that skinny boy without enough money for a granola bar, and whom he later discovered was sleeping next to his dumpster. Nikki had been surviving—the boy was still learning the difference between that and taking care.

"I only meant it was good you'd found a friend and a safe place to stay last night."

But now you need to come home.

"Oh." Nikki sighed into the phone. "Well, yeah. Brian's a good friend."

"He's a good boy. I'm glad you have him. But I am sincerely hoping you'll come home today. Perhaps you'd like to have a quiet, private dinner with me?"

Nikki snorted. "Home."

"The brownstone. Home. Yes."

"Is it home, though?"

"Isn't it?" Well. This conversation was marvelously awkward.

"I was upset. I'm still upset."

"That's okay. Upset doesn't mean you don't belong here. We both were thrown."

"Thrown?"

"Nikki. Why don't you tell me about it when you get here?" As always, he chose his words carefully. *When you get here.* Not if, *when*. "I will listen, I promise."

"But...aren't you angry?"

"I am not. Not in the least." Worried, shaken, but not angry.

"Why not?"

Goodness, the boy was hard on himself. "My boy. I have no reason to be angry with you. I've failed you, not the other way around."

"But I..."

The line went silent for a long while, and Bradford finally had to break it to save his own sanity. "Are you there?"

There was a fumbling on the line, some quiet words, and then Brian answered him.

"It's Brian, sir. Nikki is...he's...I'll bring him to you soon, Master Bradford."

"Thank you. You're a good boy, Brian. Please feel free to eat in the dining room tonight. I'll let Levi know."

"Thank you, sir. We'll see you soon, sir."

The line went dead.

Bradford hung up and looked at the phone, remembering the first intimate night he spent with Harrison. It was different certainly, as they were both Doms and they didn't play together, but the parallel was too obvious to ignore. He'd never anticipated following his husband's example—helping Nikki off the street and teaching the boy to be more than Nikki had ever imagined—but here he was. Here *they* were. He was infatuated, inspired by Nikki's progress and depth, and it felt good. It had been so long.

He called Levi back and arranged for dinner to be brought to them later and kept warm in the brownstone's comfortable kitchen; then he took a quick shower and shaved, making himself presentable for his boy.

He went to his office, thinking that was a more neutral private space than the brownstone, and Brian brought Nikki right to him, keeping protectively close behind Nikki's shoulder as Nikki approached him. The boy looked exhausted and anxious to a degree he hadn't observed since their first encounter in the coffee shop.

His palms itched. He was eager to pull Nikki to him, assure himself the boy was whole, tell Nikki how worried he'd been. But he kept his tone gentle and his hands to himself, both entirely contrary to his desire, ever the master of his own impulses. "Hello, boy."

"Hi...sir." Nikki's voice was hoarse and tired too.

He was grateful to Brian for looking after Nikki but now it was time to be alone with the boy. "Thank you for bringing him to me, Brian."

"Nikki, do you want me to stay?" *Oh. Good boy.* Bradford was so proud of Brian, but that didn't stop him from hoping that Nikki would decline.

"I'm all right, Brian. Thank you so much for everything." Nikki gave Brian a quick kiss on the cheek, and Brian hugged the boy hard.

"Call me, okay?"

"I will. Promise." The look that passed between the two subs said more than words could. Bradford respected that sort of bond.

"Good to see you, sir."

Bradford walked Brian to the door. "I'm very proud of you for being such a good friend and taking care of one of our own. Again."

Brian nodded. "It's my pleasure to be of service, sir."

"Good boy. I know. Don't forget your dinner. Good night."

"Good night, sir."

The room went still and quiet, and for a moment it felt as if Brian had taken all the oxygen with him when the boy left the room. But a moment later Nikki took a deep breath, breaking the awkward silence, and that seemed to give Bradford permission to do the same.

"I am gratified that you have come home."

"Gratified?" Nikki snorted.

"Grateful. I'm—I appreciate that you are willing to give your submission a second chance."

"I didn't say that."

He raised an eyebrow and exhaled heavily. "Very well.

What have you come home to say?" He continued, stubbornly, to use "home," determined to make it clear that he felt this was where Nikki belonged.

Nikki sat in the chair opposite his desk. "I'm not sure I know what to say. I feel...I felt...it hurt to be rejected like that, Bradford."

He went to Nikki, took the boy's hands and leaned against his desk. He noted the injury to Nikki's knuckles but thought it best not to distract the boy by mentioning it just now. He would see to it later when things were calmer. "My boy. I didn't reject you, I refused you. It's not the same thing."

"It felt like the same thing. And why do you have to...to... do *that*? You said no, Bradford. What's the difference why?"

"It's a world of difference, boy."

"I'm not your fucking *boy* right now, Bradford. I'm Nikki. Just Nikki. I'm just...who I am."

"Who you are?" He rubbed his forehead. "These aren't exclusive identities, boy. You're not trying on costumes. You are Nikki and you are a sub, and you are—"

Mine. You're mine. God, I want you.

"See? This is why I left. I don't belong here if I can't understand what you're saying to me. What you're doing." Nikki's tone was stressed, anxiety so plain.

"It's not your job to figure out how to understand, it's mine to ensure that you can." Bradford tried to be reassuring, calm, but Nikki was working himself up, shaking his head.

"I'm not like the other subs! They're all so perfect and I'm..."

"Different, Nikki. You're perfect too." He understood that; it was what had drawn him to Nikki from the beginning.

"Just say it. I know, okay? I'm a fuckup!"

He reached for Nikki, taking the boy by the shoulders despite every brain cell he possessed screaming at him not to. "You are *not* a fuckup!"

Nikki tensed and blinked at him.

"Oh, dear God, I am sorry. I didn't intend to shout at you, boy." Bradford loosened his grip on Nikki's shoulders but couldn't quite bring himself to let go entirely. "I am so terribly sorry. But you have to understand, boy. I have worked with so many subs in the club. They are all wonderful in their way. I know how it looks, but they are far from perfect. And I have never wished to call any of them— or any sub at all apart from you, for that matter—mine. You are not a fuckup. You are learning. What more could I possibly ask of you?"

Nikki was still as stone, breathing deeply and staring at him.

"Boy?"

"S...sir."

The moment felt so fragile, he almost didn't dare breathe. "Good boy. I think you should get some rest."

"Yes, sir." Nikki returned the nod and moved closer. "Thank you, Master."

Oh. Oh, what a lovely gift. Now he could breathe. Bradford inhaled deeply, the scent of his boy filling his nostrils and the warmth filling his arms.

They'd rest. And when they woke, they'd make this official. They both deserved it.

21

"I want to introduce you to Master Tobias."

"Okay. What does he do?"

Bradford gestured to the chair opposite his desk. "That's personal information. I'm sure he'll tell you all about it when he's ready."

"But...I don't know much about him." Noah sat, leaned back in the chair and crossed his legs, settling an ankle on one knee.

"So much the better."

"But...I mean, he's been MIA for a while, right? The way people talk it sounds like he's been—"

"Busy. Working hard." Bradford knew damn well that wasn't what "people," especially the longtime subs, said about Tobias. But he decided to play with Noah a bit.

Noah snorted. "A recluse."

"Really?" Well. That was probably true at the moment. He hadn't heard that term used himself, but just as Doms had their confidants, subs, when permitted, would talk as well. "No, boy. Master Tobias is no recluse." Lonely and heartbroken? Yes. Depressed for sure. Turning forty-one and in need of a new boy?

Absolutely.

Not that Tobias knew that. That was what best friends were for, right? To know these things. And as Tobias had made a reservation for dinner on the occasion of his forty-first birthday, Bradford could comfortably spring a gift on him. With any luck, Tobias would be a gift to Noah as well.

"Rumors among this community, boy, are abundant and prolific. I don't encourage them among the membership, and my advice is you ignore them. They are useless at best."

"Yes, sir."

Something about the way Noah said "Yes, sir" was so satisfying. It never felt like lip service or habit. It felt honest.

Tobias would love that. He would be drawn to the boy's sincerity, to Noah's raw need. Much like the animals that Tobias looked after day in and day out, Noah needed looking after. Tobias wouldn't be able to resist.

The boy was the perfect birthday gift.

"I want you to give him a try."

"But he's never at the club."

"No. You're right, he's been scarce of late. But he'll be here Friday night for his birthday, and I want him to meet you."

Noah sighed heavily. "Bradford, I have to tell you, I'm—"

"I know, my boy. And I'm so sorry."

"This shouldn't be so hard."

"Oh, yes." He got up and moved around the desk to sit in the vacant chair beside the boy. Noah wasn't a sub for just anyone. The depth of the boy's need and Noah's polished training deserved someone who would recognize it. "You're wrong there, boy. It should be hard. You want it to be right. It should be a hard search, but an easy decision."

Noah looked at him, searched his eyes. "You're saying I'll know...when I know."

"That is exactly what I am saying. When you meet the right man, the right Dom, you will know."

"At a certain point, I have to wonder if it's me."

Bradford shrugged. "It is you, in fact. But don't give up. I'm not. What good to you is a Dom that doesn't...click?"

"Click?"

"Like a key in a lock."

Noah laughed softly and nodded. "All right, sir. Master Tobias, on Friday."

"Don't be late, boy. He's a stickler. Be here at six."

Noah nodded. "Yes, sir."

22

Nikki lifted the note off his dresser, familiar now with the stationery. Bradford had left it for him while he was showering after work. The request was familiar too—mostly. This one had a bit of a twist.

My dear boy,

I would be honored if you would join me for dinner this evening. Come in casual and comfortable clothing, and please bring with you a notebook or journal and a pen as you may wish to take notes.

Respectfully,

Master Bradford

Take notes during dinner? Odd. But Sir loved little games like this, and Nikki had learned it was best, and wisest, to follow the Dom's instructions to the letter.

So he did.

Nikki wore soft pants and a loose T-shirt and was feeling horribly underdressed as he approached the door from Bradford's private quarters to the club. He was just thinking he should change his mind when the door opened, and

Brian smiled at him broadly. "You're here! Master Bradford asked me to come check on you."

"I'm fine. Thank you, Brian."

"Something big is happening tonight, right? He's already ordered dinner for both of you and he's reserved a room. You're so lucky."

"Thank you, Brian." He didn't know any of that until now, of course, but he wasn't going to let on.

"Master looks so good too."

"He—but he told me to be casual and comfortable."

"I'm sure he has his reasons. But see?" Brian elbowed him and gestured to where Bradford was seated with a quick nod of his head.

Bradford stood as they made their way over. The Dom did look amazing. A light-gray suit, lavender tie, hair combed perfectly, eyes warm.

So handsome.

Nikki felt horribly uncomfortable now.

"Good evening, Nikki. Thank you for joining me." Bradford stepped out from behind the table to hold his chair.

Whoa.

Nikki hesitated a second before smiling and taking a seat. "You look amazing. I look...I mean, when you told me casual and comfortable I—"

"You look perfect. You've done just as I asked. Thank you." Bradford reached for a pitcher of water on the table to fill their water glasses, and that was when Nikki noticed Brian was suddenly nowhere to be found.

"You're welcome, sir."

Bradford held a hand up. "No need for 'sir' right now. For the moment, I'd like it to be just Bradford and Nikki.

Two men having a conversation as equals. That's important."

Uh oh. Was that bad? It kind of sounded bad. Bradford was a stickler for formalities, so what did it mean that he didn't want titles used at all? "Did I do something wrong?"

"Not at all. I want to discuss a long-term arrangement with you."

"A...?" *Long-term arrangement?*

"An agreement. I'd like to negotiate a long-term agreement with you. Three months, perhaps, for starters?"

"Three months?" He sounded like an idiot, repeating everything Bradford was saying, but it felt like Bradford was miles ahead of him in the conversation already.

"Oh. Perhaps that's too long. Of course. Would you be more comfortable with a month to begin with?"

He shook his head. "Can you just...hold on. Let me catch up here. You want, like, a contract?"

Bradford smiled and leaned back in his chair. "Not quite, no...I'm so sorry. I launched into this thinking you knew what I was talking about."

"I might. I think I do, but can I just clarify?" Because he'd learned that he and Bradford did much better if he double-checked everything.

"Of course. Let me start this differently. Why don't you open your notebook?"

"Oh. Good idea." The notebook. Now he understood what it was for.

"You and I negotiate terms for every scene, right? We sit here and have dinner, I tell you what I'd like you to agree to, you have the opportunity to express your own needs and set your limits, and we specify a duration. A few hours, overnight, two days...etcetera."

"Right, okay." He nodded and wrote, "Agreement with

Bradford" at the top of the page. "So this would be negotiating but for three months?"

"Or a month, if you'd prefer shorter."

"Like when? Just weekends or something?"

"Well, I would prefer around the clock actually. Twenty-four seven."

"Around the clock like, all day?"

"And all night. Every day. For whatever duration you agree to. Assuming you agree at all, of course."

All day and all night for three months. *Whoa.* "So...the rules would apply all the time?"

"Every minute."

Nikki looked up at Bradford. "But...what if I screw up?" He was going to screw up. He knew it, and Bradford expected it. It wasn't a matter of if, but when.

"What if you do? Mistakes happen. One of the really helpful things about a long-term arrangement is that when you live as a sub every day, all day, you get lots of practice."

Nikki laughed. "I get more opportunity to make a mistake."

"That too." Bradford looked at him patiently. "But you will learn. That's the point."

He nodded slowly. That did make sense. But no one had made decisions for him since he was fourteen. He wasn't sure how he felt about it now. "I have questions."

"So, ask them."

"How serious is this?"

"Very serious. I would consider it binding, like any other gentleman's agreement."

Binding, he wrote in his notebook. "What if we're two weeks in and it's not working?"

"Well, we can amend as needed, though you don't want to mess with it too much."

Okay. So he had an out, and the ability to change the deal if he really needed to. But what about— "Do I get... time off?"

"Time...off." Bradford repeated it like the words didn't make any sense.

"Yeah. Like if I want to go out to a movie or to a bar with friends or something."

"Ah. Personal time. Yes, of course. You are still under contract when we are not physically together, such as at work, or on personal time. All you need to do, however, is ask."

"Ask?"

"Exactly. Ask for my permission."

Wait. What? "I need your permission to see friends?"

"Yes and no. You will see your friends, but it will require my permission for you to see friends at a particular time. You need to be sure I don't have other plans for you. As in a scene, my needs would remain your constant priority. You would be mine, first and foremost."

He squinted at Bradford. "So, are you going to say no?"

Bradford snorted softly and shook his head. "I don't intend to hold you hostage, Nikki."

Shit. "I didn't mean...I know. I'm sorry."

Bradford leaned forward, reached across the table, and took his hand. "There's no need to apologize. This is all new to you and I understand your concern. If you'd like to try this, let's agree on a month for now. That ought to be long enough for you get a taste of full-time service without trapping you in something we might have to dissolve. That would be terribly discouraging."

Nikki chewed his lip thoughtfully. He wanted to learn more, but he wasn't interested in working with anyone else. Bradford took everything slow—sometimes it even felt too slow—and he thought they had a real trust between them. If he was going to try this with anyone, Bradford was the right choice.

There were full-time subs under long-term contracts all over the club. There were experienced subs like Noah and Cade who were actively looking for contracts and hadn't found them. Bradford was offering *him* that chance. He was curious. He wanted to know.

"Okay. I'll agree to a month-long contract."

Bradford squeezed his hand and sat back again. "I'm glad to hear that. But, to be clear, I'm not offering an actual contract. I'm not sure either of us is ready for that yet. I'd like to make it a formal agreement on a handshake."

"No contract? But isn't that what everybody does?"

"It's customary at a certain level, yes. But a simple agreement will allow us to build trust. We have to put faith in each other's word."

Nikki thought about that. "I have to trust your word…"

"Exactly so. And I will trust yours. It calls upon our integrity and our continued desire to work together, instead of being bound by and falling back on a signature."

Oh, he knew what was happening now. "It's a test."

"No, boy." Bradford squinted at him. "It's a show of faith."

God, this man and his *words*. "What's the difference?"

"The difference is that you will have the right to point out my mistakes without the need for a safe word. When we're not in a formal scene, where of course you would always have full use of your safe words, we could adjust and fine-tune when necessary, with an eye toward a contract in the future."

"Oh. Oh, I get it. So we can talk a lot about what's happening and not have to negotiate all over again."

Bradford gave him an approving smile. "Do you want to start with what you want, or should I?"

Did he know what he wanted? "You start."

Bradford nodded. "Very well. For the period of one month, I would like you to be mine full-time, night and day. I will teach you about long-term service. I will see to all of your needs—the obvious ones such as food and rest, and the less obvious, which we'll discover together in-scene and elsewhere. I will offer you an opportunity every day to speak your mind freely so we can negotiate further and fine-tune —perhaps even experiment. As your Dom, I demand your devotion, and as my sub, I expect you to learn to anticipate me and to put my needs and desires before your own." Bradford stopped talking and watched him. "How does that sound so far?"

It sounded like Bradford really wanted to take care of him. He wasn't used to that, and it made his chest ache a little. "Good. So far, good."

Bradford nodded. "Very well. I would like to establish some limits now, so we don't have questions come up that will interrupt our rhythm. I know we're still discovering your pain limits and your interests in-scene, and I will continue to take that slowly and carefully as we have been."

"Can we fuck?" He blinked as the words just popped out. *Jesus, Nikki.*

Bradford blinked right back at him, and he smiled slightly. "I was getting to that, but as long as we're there, yes. I would like sex, without restrictions, to be on the table."

"Without restrictions?"

"Well, you can set your boundaries of what you'll allow, but I want intercourse and oral to be specifically addressed. I'd like to keep things like rough sex and sex while restrained on the table. You can always end anything that makes you uncomfortable with a safe word. I will always use protection, of course."

Rough sex? Jesus Christ. Was he supposed to be turned-on during a negotiation? "Sure. Fine. Sex is on the table. Without restrictions."

A knowing grin pulled at the corner Bradford's lips. "Thank you for that trust, Nikki. I promise to be worthy of it."

He nodded. He did trust Bradford. With everything.

And he was really into rough sex.

"I'm demanding, Nikki. But I promise you I'll do everything I can to reward your devotion. Whatever your needs, I will meet them, as I believe I have done to this point; Brian and Levi are entirely different subs, but I work well with each of them. Feel free to speak with them any time."

"About that..." He got to ask for things, too, right?

"About?"

"Levi and Brian and...all those overnight subs."

Bradford smiled slowly. "What are you asking, Nikki?"

Dammit. Bradford was going to make him say it? "If I'm yours then...then you're mine."

"Of course."

"Twenty-four seven."

"Indeed." Bradford leaned back in his chair.

Nikki sighed. *Fine.* "I want us to be exclusive in everything. Including sex."

"Ah." Bradford took a sip of water, looking thoughtful. "I will not have intimate relations with any other sub during the term of our agreement. However, it happens that part of my job is the well-being and suitability of our subs. I need to know all of them—how they work, what they need. And some of them I work with regularly. I have to ask that you understand the difference between my work and my personal time with you."

Right. Noah, Phan, Brian, Cade, Levi...Bradford worked with all of them. "Work, okay. But when you're not working...can we not have other subs here all night? Would that be okay? And you won't bring Levi home, right?"

Bradford took his hand. "I hear you, boy. Outside of work, you would be my sub exclusively. In everything. I hadn't thought about the overnight help, but of course I will suspend that practice as I will have no need of them. And I won't have the need, or the desire for anyone else in my bed."

Okay, then. He took a deep breath and smiled, knowing he'd been heard. "I guess the only thing I really need then is your patience."

Bradford smiled, the look happy and lighting up his eyes. "You have it already. That won't change."

He wrote the words "EXCLUSIVE" and "PATIENCE" in big capital letters in his notes, then took another breath, trying to quiet the anxiety and arousal and excitement all churning in his stomach. "I feel kind of wound-up. Am I supposed to be nervous?"

"That means you understand this is a big step, Nikki. Nervous, excited, worried, curious, hopeful...there are no wrong emotions here. Unless you're scared. Fear should not enter into this equation."

"No. No, I'm not scared. I want to try this."

"When would you like to start? I'm ready right this moment, but I've been thinking about this for a few days. If you'd like to sleep on it, I absolutely respect that."

He didn't need to sleep on it. All he'd do was stay up all night anxious—anxious about being exclusive, anxious about the future, and anxious to get started. "Now is good."

"All right." Bradford offered a hand across the table. "Shake on it, then come kneel by my chair and we'll have an agreement."

"Kneel?" That was so awkward the last time.

"It's a custom here at the club when a Dom and a sub come to a formal agreement."

"Will people—" Bradford always drew so many eyes. "Again?"

"I apologize, but we will likely get a bit of attention, yes. Try to keep your eyes low and your mind focused on me."

He was hoping that if he did this enough, if he stood up in front of people, if people looked at him enough, he'd get used to it.

He would, right? He had to. Eventually.

He hoped.

His heart was pounding as he took Bradford's hand and shook it. He stood and moved to Bradford's side, keeping his eyes on the pristine wood floor, and carefully sank to his knees next to Bradford's chair.

Someone called out, "Congratulations!" and the sentiment was echoed around the dining room with light applause and knives clinking against wineglasses.

Bradford reached down and rested a hand on his shoulder. "Good boy. They are as proud of you as I am."

That was fine, but Bradford was the only man in the world he wanted to make proud beside himself.

Bradford gave a wave and the room went quiet again. "So, boy. Tell me, are you hungry? Or would you prefer to get out from under all these eyes and pay a visit to my St. Andrew's cross?"

He was actually feeling okay, kneeling there with Bradford. But he wasn't hungry, and he didn't think he could eat right now anyway. He was too excited. Too curious. And way too eager for Bradford's attention.

"I'm ready if you're ready, sir."

"I'm ready. At my heel, then, eyes low. Remember, I'm proud of you, boy. The only opinion in this room that matters is mine. I'll move quickly."

"Yes, sir."

The only opinion in this room that matters is mine.

Could it really be that simple?

Bradford stood and Nikki joined him, following hard on his Master's heel, eyes low.

The only opinion that matters is his.

And Bradford was proud.

Nikki finally got it. He'd just come to an agreement with the *owner* of the club.

With Master Bradford.

He kept his eyes low, but he lifted his chin and straightened his shoulders. He was Master Bradford's boy. Fuck if he wasn't proud too.

The rest of the dining room disappeared as he focused on matching Bradford's stride, and he discovered it really could be that easy. He had a Master to please. His Master. He didn't have time to worry about who was judging him.

Bradford stopped outside the room and handed him the key. He took it, opened the door, and held it.

"Good boy. Hang the key up, then strip as usual and kneel." Bradford went to the intercom on the wall and checked in with security while Nikki undressed. He folded his clothes and set them on the table by the door, then went to the middle of the room and settled into kneeling display. He closed his eyes and listened to Bradford move around the room, concentrating on what he wanted to give his Master.

"Safe words, please, boy."

"Nickel and dime, sir."

" 'Nickel and dime.' I expect you to use them, boy. You and I are learning each other. We're only human, yes? It's entirely possible you will need them tonight."

"Yes, sir. I will use them if I—" *If I know I need them? Will I know?* "Sir, what if—may I ask a question, sir?"

"Of course. Tonight you have my permission to ask questions any time you like, all right?"

Oh, that was helpful. "Thank you, sir. What if I don't know if I need to use a safe word?"

"If you're unsure, then the answer is always yes. Better to err on the side of caution. Use 'nickel' and we'll talk about it."

"If I'm not sure, then...oh, that makes sense, sir, thank you."

"Remember." Bradford rested a hand on the back of his head, and Nikki leaned into it. "You can't disappoint me if you're doing your best, boy."

He nodded. "Thank you, sir."

"On your feet, boy." Sir moved away and he stood. A second later, his Master was behind him again, crowding close, bare chest warm against his back. "To the cross. We both deserve to get what we want tonight."

"Sir." His heart started pounding and he forgot to move, but Sir herded him along, maneuvering him right to the cross. Sir's hands touched him all over as they buckled him in, securing his hands and feet; then the falls of a flogger began to land lightly on his ass.

"I'm going to give you a little of my arm, boy. Give you stripes you won't forget for a couple of days. And..." The flogger fell harder and in moments their touch became a sharp sting. "I will have you."

Fuck, yes. Please. His balls drew up tight, making him moan, and his Master hummed approval in response. "Mmm. You like that, boy?"

"Yes, sir."

Bradford took in a sharp breath behind him. "Shoulders now. Don't forget your safe words. I'm listening."

Sir started in slow, the flogger's blows only warming his skin at first. Over and over they fell on his shoulders, intensifying until they burned just right. His breathing grew shallow but steady, in and out with the rhythm of his Master's arm.

"Beautiful boy." The blows stopped and Sir stepped up beside him.

He took a deep, deep breath and let it out. "Master." God, he wasn't ready. Close but...it wasn't enough. "More. Please."

He felt Bradford studying him. "Are you sure, boy?"

He nodded. "Need you. Please."

"Very well. A few more. Good boy." Sir's warmth disappeared but it was replaced by his Master's strong, commanding voice. "Harder, boy. We'll try four and see where we are. Breathe. Tell me when you're ready."

Nikki breathed in and out, focusing on his Master. "Ready, sir."

"Four in a row and we'll breathe again. Breathe."

He heard the first blow before he felt it; then the four blows seared his skin like fire, making him rock against the cross and cry out.

"Boy?" Master was at his side again.

"Sir. Oh, God. So good."

Bradford's hand landed on his belly, fingers hot and burning almost as much as the flogger had. He moaned and leaned into the touch. He breathed in deep and this time when he exhaled, he felt different.

New.

Clean.

"Master."

Sir's voice was rough, but his reply was clear. "My boy."

"Yours, Master." The hand on his belly moved lower, fingers curling around his shaft. Oh God, he ached. "Want you."

"Mine. My boy."

He loved the way his Master's words dissolved into a growl at the end. He let himself beg and pushed through Sir's fingers. He had no shame. Everything he was belonged to his Master now.

"Please, sir."

His Master moved away, and he floated for a minute. Or an hour. He just couldn't tell.

———

"My good boy." Bradford watched Nikki as he slowly rolled on a condom, taking in the way the boy moved, the way that lean body swayed and arched, begging for his attention. He found the warmer and pumped some lube into one hand and made his way back over to his boy.

His boy.

Finally.

Soon to be even more his own.

He gripped Nikki by one hip and tucked his slippery fingers tightly up against his boy's hole. He wasn't wasting another second. "We've waited long enough."

"Yes, sir. Please, yes." Nikki arched into his touch and took his fingers right in, the move making his mouth go dry.

"Needy boy."

"Yes. Oh, God." Nikki rode his fingers, rocking and arching, and he allowed it. It was the hottest fucking thing he'd seen in ages. But his abs were tight and his balls ached, and he wasn't going to let the boy be indulgent for long. He knew what he wanted—what they both needed.

He had every intention of getting it.

He leaned over Nikki's striped back, letting the boy feel the heat and get a taste of his aching cock against that lovely, pale ass. "Going to take you, my boy. Are you ready for me?"

Nikki practically howled for him. "Sir! Yes, so ready. Oh, God."

He withdrew his fingers and replaced them with the head of his swollen prick. He'd had every intention of making this first connection slowly, easing the boy into things. But Nikki had other ideas. He'd just started to push past the boy's entrance, had only just nudged that tight ring of muscle, when Nikki rocked hard and took him in deep.

"Boy!" He shouted, both hands taking hold of Nikki's hips for balance until he could breathe again and his brain was back in the game.

Oh, he did love a naughty boy.

He let Nikki ride another second, then shoved the boy against the cross, pinning him there with hard thrusts. Nikki grunted and gave him a little bit of a struggle, which only made everything sweeter.

"Mine, boy." Bradford's breathing was ragged and his voice was rough.

"Sir! More!"

He'd been careful of the boy's back, but now he leaned right up against it, his chest pressing against the hot stripes. Nikki let out a long cry but never gave him a hint of a safe word, the boy's ass arching toward him, begging for more.

A few more hard thrusts and his own climax started to twist and coil in his gut. His boy was babbling to him and trembling now, sweating and hard to keep a grip on. Bradford pulled back on Nikki's hip and slipped a hand around the boy's pretty cock, and that was all it took. Nikki shook and shot hard, hips jerking and the muscles around him contracting.

They both groaned and panted; then Bradford followed Nikki over the cliff, pumping inside his boy.

They hung there a moment, high as kites, flying on hormones and endorphins as he marveled at Nikki's unexpected depth. He'd laid into the boy pretty hard at the end, and Nikki had never once seemed anywhere near a safe word. They had so much to explore together and he was looking forward to all of it.

They couldn't remain standing there long; he had responsibilities. Almost as soon as he'd had that thought, Nikki's knees buckled. Bradford caught him and set him against the cross.

"I've got you, boy. Feet first." He quickly unbuckled Nikki's feet and went for the boy's wrists. As soon as Nikki was free the boy moved into his arms, leaning heavily.

"Sir. Master," Nikki babbled as Bradford moved him to the divan and stretched him out on his stomach.

"Such a good boy. My good boy." He offered soft words in return and a gentle tone as he disposed of his condom and began his aftercare routine. He pulled over a stool and sat as he carefully applied ointment to the beautiful stripes on Nikki's back. Only a few had cut into the skin, but Nikki would be sore for a couple of days.

Nikki sighed at his touch. "Thank you, sir."

"I can't wait for you to see your back, boy. How do you feel?"

"Good. So good, sir. I've never...I...I don't have words."

Bradford smiled and bent to kiss Nikki's cheek affectionately. "That's all right, my boy. As long as you feel good."

Sometimes words came later, and sometimes there just weren't any.

Bradford felt as if his own feelings might fall into the latter category.

EPILOGUE

"Everything all right, Timmy?"

"Yes, Master Bradford. You wanted to know when Master Tobias arrived. His car just pulled up."

"Oh. Wonderful. Thank you." Timmy was calling from the valet desk. Bradford could hear the street noise through the phone.

"My pleasure, sir."

Bradford grinned as he hung up the phone. Timmy was such a good boy. He got up from his desk and made his way out to the foyer, arriving just in time. He opened the door to welcome his oldest friend, mentor, and confidant, Tobias Vincent.

"Tobias! Timothy said you were here." Forty-one years looked good on the Dom. He was as handsome as ever and owned it.

Tobias shook his head and smiled. "I trust you don't mind me appearing again after all this time?"

Bradford met him on the steps and shook his hand. "The day we turn you from here, my friend, is the day I close the old place up. Now, come in! Eat. Enjoy your birthday. I have a room reserved for you, as you requested. You're not meeting anyone, are you?"

Tobias shook his head again and was looking around the foyer and into the bar area. "I don't have a guest, if that's what you mean, but I'm open to possibilities."

"I was hoping you would say that." He gave Tobias a long look. "In which case..."

"Wait," Tobias said, laughing. "I'm not saying I want you to find me a date. I'm just saying I want to have a pleasant evening—a nice meal, people I like around me—"

Oh, please. How long had they known each other? Bradford knew better than that. A Dom wanted a sub. Needed one, in point of fact. "And it's been eight months since you've been here, Tobias. I know you spend your weekends on the farm and your weeknights in town. I'd certainly have heard if you had someone new." He shook his head sadly, making Tobias grin. "No, my friend, you deserve to play. And I might just have the right someone for you."

Bradford had been so excited when Tobias had finally said he was going to have dinner at the club. It had been so long. It was time to let the past go. And the Dom's timing couldn't have been better.

"Tell me," Tobias invited, accepting a glass of ice water from the bartender.

Bradford beamed at him, delighted. "I can do you one better. Come."

Bradford led Tobias through the bar to a small table where he'd asked Noah to sit and wait for him. The boy rose quickly as they approached.

"Tobias." He swept an arm toward Noah. "I would like you to meet Noah. Noah, this is Tobias. It is my opinion that the two of you are well suited. Of course, you may decide otherwise, but I encourage you to at least discuss the matter."

He had no intention of staying for more than introductions. He knew Tobias needed to be a little off-balance for this to work. Bradford bowed his head and stepped back, wishing them a good evening before turning and walking away, leaving Tobias and Noah on their own.

Enjoyed Soft Limits? Try First Rodeo!

First Rodeo
The Cowboy and the Dom Trilogy, Book One
By Jodi Payne and BA Tortuga
https://jodipayne.net/books/first-rodeo/

When a killer strikes, Texan and former rodeo cowboy, Sam O'Reilly, loses his older brother. Unbeknownst to Sam, James was also the lover and sub of a sophisticated New York City Dom named Thomas Ward. Sam comes to the city determined to stay until he can bring the murderer to his own brand of justice, while Thomas' more ordered mind is hoping for a legal solution. Neither man expects their connection to the other, but having each lost someone irreplaceable, their hearts are crying out for comfort almost as loudly as their bodies are screaming for each other.

Some yearnings refuse to be ignored, but transcending their differences to explore the fragile connection between them will prove to be a steep a hill to climb--the first of many. As Sam and Thomas take the first tentative steps on the rocky path that might lead to a relationship, the killer steps out of the shadows...

And this time, his sights are set on Sam.

———

Breaking the Rules
The Triskelion Series, Book One
By Jodi Payne and BA Tortuga

https://jodipayne.net/books/breaking-the-rules/

Saul Reynolds manages a busy bicycle shop in downtown Boulder, Colorado. A recent CU graduate, he's also a Dom, and has many friends his age in the scene. Saul's an old soul, and even at twenty-five, he's had enough experience to understand his own desires. He's had plenty of lovers and he's played the role of part-time Dom, but he's never found the perfect combination of lover and sub in one man.

Troy Finch lost his lover in a rodeo accident twenty years ago, moved to Boulder, and has worked as a line cook in his friend Carter's diner ever since. He's attended many parties at Carter's home with couples in the BDSM lifestyle and feels comfortable in a submissive role, but without a Dom of his own, Troy hasn't explored what that really means to him. He has needs he doesn't entirely understand and finds his only outlet at the hands of Carter's husband, Geoff, a tattoo artist who has used Troy's skin as a canvas for as long as they've known each other, covering Troy in colorful, intricate triskelia.

Troy doesn't know what he was thinking accepting a dinner invitation from a kid half his age, but everything feels right about their evening together, including Saul's Dominant side. The rules for a twenty-five year old gay cowboy from years ago, though, are totally different than for a twenty-five year old college grad in Boulder now, and despite Saul's confidence, Troy isn't sure whether they can make it work.

Saul and Troy manage to bend a good many rules in the name of caring and compromise, but in the name of love, there are some rules they're just going to have to break.

This is a "true series" and should be read in order.

———

Interested in learning more about Jodi's books? Want free fiction, release news, anecdotes, coffee and drink recipes...?
Join Jodi's newsletter!
What's Up with Jodi?
http://bit.ly/whatsupjodi

THE DEVIATIONS SERIES

Book One: Submission
Read for yourself where it all started!

Tobias is a skilled Dom, able to bring even the most hesitant submissive around. Noah is a man in need of just that. He wants to sub desperately but has yet to find someone he believes can take him where he needs to go.

Through a series of encounters in the world of bondage and discipline, Noah reveals why he has trouble trusting, why he needs such a firm, steady hand. Tobias may allow himself to dominate, but he has trouble letting himself love. Still, Tobias can't resist Noah's charms, and the two of them set about making a life for themselves, one that works for them and their unique set of problems. They learn to love, but can they stay together while they explore each others' secrets, in a world where all is laid bare and emotions run high?

From authors Chris Owen and Jodi Payne comes a romance on the deviant side, where love is all tied up with the need to submit, the need to dominate, and the need to share a life of exploration and care. These two skilled authors create a world that's hard to resist, and a book that's even harder to put down.

A NOTE FROM JODI

Hey there!

I just wanted to take a minute to say thank you for taking the time to read Soft Limits. I hope you enjoyed it. I know everyone is busy and our TBR (to be read) lists are out of control, so it means a lot to me that I ended up at the top of your pile this time.

If you have a moment, please consider dropping by the site where you purchased this book and leaving a review. All honest reviews are much appreciated.

If you're looking for more of my work, why not join my newsletter? Just go here: http://bit.ly/whatsupjodi.

Thank you for reading!

Jodi

ABOUT JODI PAYNE

You're gonna love this guy...

JODI takes herself way too seriously and has been known to randomly break out in song. Her men are imperfect but genuine, stubborn but likable, often kinky, and frequently their own worst enemies. They are characters you can't help but fall in love with while they stumble along the path to their happily ever after. For those looking to get on her good side, Jodi's addictions include nonfat lattes, Malbec and tequila any way you pour it.

Website: jodipayne.net
Newsletter: http://bit.ly/whatsupjodi
All Jodi's Social Links: linktr.ee/jodipayne

ALSO BY JODI PAYNE

MM and Gay Romance

A Whole Latke Love

Soft Limits: A Deviations Novel

Stable Hill

Creative Process

Linchpin

Whence He Came

With BA Tortuga

Heart of a Redneck

Land of Enchantment

Wrecked

Window Dressing

Flying Blind

Special Delivery, A Wrecked Novel - *Coming November 2020!*

The Cowboy and the Dom Trilogy

First Rodeo, Book One

Razor's Edge, Book Two

No Ghosts, Book Three

The Soldier and the Angel

The Collaborations Series

Refraction

Syncopation